The Hollowed Realms: The Soulbound Curse

By: J.B. Grimm

The Soulbound Curse

Book One of the Hallowed Realms Saga

© 2025 J.B. Grimm

Illustrations and Visual Direction by Nell Royale

Published by Regal Insight Consulting, LLC

Tulsa, Oklahoma

www.regal-insight-consulting.online

ISBN: 979-8-9992275-3-9

Printed in the United States of America

First Edition

Dedication

To the restless spirits of the North, the wind-whipped shores of forgotten islands, and the echoes of battles long past. This tale is woven from the threads of your legends, your strength, and your sorrows. May it serve as a testament to the enduring power of the human spirit, the unwavering bonds of loyalty, and the courage to face the shadows that dance on the edge of the world. It is also dedicated to those who have ever felt the sting of isolation, the weight of the past, and the burden of a destiny they never chose. This story is for you, for your resilience, for your fight against the darkness, and for your enduring hope, even in the face of seemingly insurmountable odds. It is a dedication to the quiet heroes, the unsung warriors, those who find strength in unlikely places and forge their own paths, even when the world seems determined to push them down. May their struggles and triumphs resonate within the heart of this tale, reminding us that even in the darkest hours, the human spirit can not only survive but truly triumph. For it is in the crucible of hardship that we truly discover our mettle and the strength of our bonds. It is a testament to the fierce warriors who have fought for their people and their beliefs, and to the enduring strength of those who carry their memories forward, shaping the future through their courage. May the spirit of the ancient Vikings, with their unyielding bravery and profound loyalty, resonate throughout the pages of this story, illuminating the path of hope and determination that leads to victory against overwhelming darkness. This tale is for the dreamers, the warriors at heart, the courageous, the defiant. It is a celebration of humanity's capacity to overcome challenges that seem unconquerable, and a promise that even in the face of the greatest odds, the flame of hope can never be fully extinguished. May your journey through these pages be filled with the thrill of adventure, the comfort of friendship, and the inspiration that comes from facing and conquering our own inner demons.

Chapter 1: Discovery of the Locket

The air hung thick and heavy with the scent of dust and decay. Sunlight, weak and hesitant, filtered through a grimy attic window, illuminating motes of dust dancing in the silent space. Elias, a young man perpetually shrouded in the shadows of his own solitude, moved cautiously through the debris-strewn expanse. His grandfather, a man he barely knew, a figure more myth than memory, had passed away, leaving behind a house filled with the ghosts of a life Elias never shared. Now, he was tasked with sorting through the remnants, a grim duty that felt like sifting through the ashes of a forgotten past.

He stumbled over a discarded trunk, its wood warped and groaning under the weight of time. He pushed it aside, revealing a dark corner choked with forgotten relics. His hand brushed against something cold and metallic, half-buried beneath a pile of moth-eaten textiles. He pulled it free, his fingers tracing the intricate carvings that adorned its surface. It was a locket, small and ornate, fashioned from a dark metal that seemed to absorb the scant light. Runes, ancient and unfamiliar, snaked across its surface, whispering of forgotten languages and lost histories.

A chill, sharper than the autumn air filtering through the cracked window panes, snaked down Elias's spine. The locket felt strangely alive in his hand, pulsing with a faint, almost imperceptible energy that hummed beneath his fingertips. It wasn't just cold; it was frigid, a glacial coldness that seeped into his bones, drawing a sharp gasp from his lips. It felt...wrong, yet undeniably compelling. An irresistible force tugged at him, drawing him towards its unsettling power. He felt a strange kinship with the object, a resonance that transcended the simple act of physical contact.

Elias, a solitary figure accustomed to the silent company of his own thoughts, felt a surge of unfamiliar emotions – a yearning, a curiosity, a sense of something...missing. His life had been a tapestry woven from threads of loneliness and alienation. He felt like a ship adrift at sea, tossed about by the relentless currents of indifference, a lone wanderer searching for a harbour he couldn't name. And in this forgotten corner of his grandfather's attic, amongst the dust and decay, he felt the faintest whisper of hope, a subtle promise of something...more. The locket, cold and ancient, seemed to offer him a lifeline, a connection to something beyond his isolated existence.

He examined the locket more closely, turning it over in his hands. The metal felt strangely heavy for its size, its weight disproportionate to its dimensions. The runes, etched with a precision that spoke of a masterful hand, seemed to shift and shimmer slightly in the dim light, as if alive and breathing. He felt a faint vibration emanating from within, a subtle thrumming that resonated deep within his chest, stirring something ancient and dormant within his soul.

He cautiously opened the locket. Inside, nestled within a tarnished velvet lining, were two miniature portraits, painted with a skill that belied their age. They depicted five fierce-looking Viking warriors, their faces etched with lines of battle and hardship, their eyes burning with an intensity that seemed to pierce through the veil of time. They were clad in furs and leather, wielding weapons that spoke of brutal efficiency. Around their necks were similar lockets, smaller versions of the one Elias held.

As he gazed upon the portraits, a wave of dizziness washed over him. The images swam before his eyes, blurring into a chaotic whirlwind of swirling colors and distorted shapes. The air grew heavy, oppressive, the silence of the attic broken only by the frantic pounding of his own heart. The faint hum emanating from the locket intensified, resonating deep within his very being. He felt a pressure building in his head, a growing sense of disorientation, as if his mind were being pulled in countless different directions.

Then, the visions began.

He was no longer in the dusty attic. He was standing on a windswept island, shrouded in a thick, impenetrable fog. The air was filled with the stench of salt and blood, the cries of men, the clash of steel on steel. He saw it all with horrifying clarity: a brutal, savage massacre. Five Viking warriors, their faces mirroring the portraits in the locket, fought with desperate courage against a shadowy horde of enemies. Their weapons flashed in the gloom, their movements precise and deadly, but they were outnumbered, overwhelmed. He saw the fall of each warrior, their lives extinguished in a torrent of blood and violence. He felt the chilling bite of their fear, the agonizing sting of their wounds, the despairing coldness of death itself.

The visions were excruciatingly real, impossibly vivid. He smelled the coppery tang of blood, felt the sting of the icy sea wind on his face, heard the screams of the dying echoing across the water. He was there, a silent, horrified witness to a carnage that unfolded centuries ago. It was brutal, merciless, a testament to the merciless nature of war and the fleeting nature of life.

When the visions finally subsided, Elias collapsed onto the dusty attic floor, his body drenched in a cold sweat, his mind reeling from the shock. The locket lay open in his hand, its metallic coldness a stark reminder of the brutal reality he had just witnessed. He felt the aftershocks of the visions reverberating through him, a deep, visceral ache that settled in his bones. He wasn't just witnessing these events; he was feeling them, experiencing them as if they had happened to him, as if the memories of these warriors had somehow become intertwined with his own.

He looked at his hands, his gaze lingering on the newly defined muscles that seemed to have sprung forth overnight. He felt a newfound strength, a raw power pulsing beneath his skin. His senses were heightened, sharper, more alert. He could smell the faintest trace of dust and mildew from across the room, hear the distant murmur of traffic from the street below. His eyes felt like they could pierce the darkness, his perception enhanced beyond anything he had ever experienced. The transformation was startling, terrifying, and intoxicating all at once. He was different, stronger, changed. He had become a vessel for the souls of the fallen Vikings, their spirits merging with his own, imbuing him with their strength, their memories, their very essence.

The unsettling hum of the locket continued, a constant reminder of the ancient power that now resided within him. And as the final image of the massacre faded, a chilling realization dawned upon him: the sorceress, Morwen, was returning. He could feel her presence, a dark, malevolent energy that snaked across the miles, its tendrils of shadow reaching out to him, claiming him as her own. The fight had begun, and he, Elias, the solitary outcast, was at the center of it. His quiet, ordinary life was irrevocably shattered, replaced by a destiny he never asked for, a fight for survival against a darkness that threatened not only his own life, but potentially the fate of the world itself. The locket, a cold, ancient vessel, was his key, his burden, his destiny. The game had begun.

Chapter 2: First Visions of the Massacre

The visions slammed into him like icy waves, each one more brutal than the last. He wasn't merely an observer; he was immersed, experiencing the chilling reality of the massacre as if he were one of the warriors himself. The fog, thick and oppressive, clung to him like a shroud, muffling the sounds of battle into a distorted, echoing symphony of pain and death. He saw them clearly – five Viking warriors, their faces etched with the same fierce determination reflected in the miniature portraits within the locket. Bjorn, the leader, a mountain of a man with a beard like tangled black iron, roared a war cry that was swallowed by the fog, yet somehow resonated deep within Elias's soul. Olaf, his axe a blur of deadly motion, carved a path through the shadowy figures that swarmed around them. Leif, his shield a battered testament to countless battles, fought with the stoicism of a seasoned veteran. And then there were Ragnar and Harald, twins, whose movements were as synchronized as the tides, their swords a deadly dance of death.

Their enemies were formless, shadowy figures, their faces obscured by the gloom, their motives unknowable. But their savagery was undeniable. They moved with unnatural speed and precision, their attacks relentless, their purpose wicked. They were like wraiths, born of darkness, fuelled by something ancient and malevolent. Elias felt the chilling bite of their weapons, the searing pain of their strikes, the bone-jarring impact of their blows. He saw Bjorn fall, his final roar choked by a tide of black blood. He saw Olaf's axe shatter against an unseen force, his body collapsing under the weight of countless blows. He witnessed Leif's shield crumble, his valiant defence finally overwhelmed by sheer numbers. Ragnar and Harald fell together, their bodies intertwined in a final, desperate embrace, their lives extinguished in a single, brutal flurry of shadows and steel.

The screams of the dying men were a deafening chorus, a horrific symphony of agony that resonated even in the hushed silence of the attic. Elias felt the cold grip of fear, the icy terror that constricted his breath, the numbing despair that stole the air from his lungs. The ground beneath his feet felt unstable; the very air itself seemed to vibrate with the intensity of the spectral violence. He was there, caught in the vortex of the massacre, a helpless witness to the merciless slaughter that unfolded around him. He saw the blood, the guts, the mangled bodies – the raw horror of battle stripped bare. He felt it, smelled it, tasted the metallic tang of death on his tongue.

The visions weren't just images; they were visceral experiences, shattering his senses, assaulting his very being. His body trembled uncontrollably, his heart pounding a frantic rhythm against his ribs, his breath coming in ragged gasps. He felt a profound sense of loss, a grief so intense it threatened to overwhelm him. The lives of these warriors, these strangers separated from him by centuries, were now inextricably bound to his own. He bore witness not only to their deaths but to their courage, their resilience, their unwavering spirit in the face of overwhelming odds.

The visions finally subsided, leaving him crumpled on the dusty floor, his body slick with sweat, his mind reeling from the sheer intensity of the experience. The silence of the attic pressed in around him, amplifying the frantic thudding of his heart. He lay there for a long time, his mind struggling to process the horrifying spectacle he had just witnessed, his senses still ringing with the echo of screams. The air was thick, heavy, laden with the lingering scent of salt, blood, and the unseen terrors of the fog-shrouded island.

He was no longer just Elias, the solitary outcast. He was Elias, the vessel, the conduit, the unwilling recipient of five Viking souls. He felt their presence within him, a powerful force that hummed beneath his skin, a torrent of memories, emotions, and experiences flooding his consciousness. Their strength coursed through his veins, their fighting skills instinctively imprinted on his mind, their rage and sorrow a constant undercurrent beneath his own emotions.

Yet, beneath the hum of warrior souls, Elias sensed something else— fainter, deeper, a presence that did not speak but watched. Unlike the Viking spirits, it didn't press forward or guide him. It remained still, as if waiting. Elias couldn't explain the chill that danced along his spine or the flicker of unease that passed through his thoughts. He pushed the feeling aside, telling himself it was just the locket's power... but somewhere in the corners of his mind, he knew. The locket had not revealed everything.

He sat up slowly, feeling the strange new strength in his limbs, a power that seemed to defy the limitations of his previous physique. His muscles felt taut and responsive, his body hardened, his reflexes sharper. He looked down at his hands, noticing the callous on his palms, the corded muscles in his forearms, the strength that now resided within his seemingly frail frame. He hadn't just witnessed the massacre; he had lived it. He had become something more, something other, something...ancient.

A profound sense of unease settled in his gut. This power, this connection to the fallen Vikings, was a double-edged sword. It granted him incredible strength and capabilities, but it also burdened him with their memories, their traumas, their unresolved fates. He felt the weight of their deaths pressing down on him, a somber responsibility, a profound connection to the past. The locket, nestled in his hand, was more than just an artifact; it was a vessel, a conduit, a living link to the brutal history it contained. It pulsed faintly, a steady rhythm that echoed the beat of his own heart, a constant reminder of the power it held, the darkness it concealed, and the destiny it imposed.

The visions had shown him the past, but a chilling premonition of the future began to take shape. He sensed an encroaching darkness, a malevolent presence growing stronger, its icy tendrils stretching across the miles, reaching out to claim him. He knew, with a certainty that chilled him to the bone, that the sorceress, Morwen, was returning. Her presence was a palpable thing, an oppressive weight that threatened to crush him, a looming shadow that promised unimaginable destruction.

The whispers of the runes on the locket, once a mystery, now began to form a chilling narrative, a prophecy foretold. The massacre was not just a historical event; it was a harbinger of things to come. The return of the sorceress was no coincidence; it was a consequence, an inevitable culmination of events set in motion centuries ago. The five Vikings, their souls trapped within the locket, were not merely victims;

they were guardians, protectors against a darkness that threatened to consume the world. And Elias, the unlikely vessel, was their last hope. The fight was far from over; it was just beginning. The stakes were impossibly high; the fate of the world rested on his shoulders. He closed the locket, the weight of his new reality pressing down on him. The cold metal felt oddly comforting, a stark reminder of the awesome task that lay ahead. The game, as they say, had truly begun.

The transformation wasn't gradual; it was a violent, visceral upheaval. One moment, Elias was weak, his body trembling from the aftermath of the visions; the next, a searing heat erupted within him, spreading through his veins like wildfire. His muscles, once soft and undefined, bulged and hardened, the contours of his body reshaping themselves with alarming speed. He felt bones shift and realign, a deep, resonant cracking echoing in his ears, a symphony of change that was both terrifying and exhilarating. His skin tingled, his pores opening to release a torrent of sweat, leaving him slick and glistening in the dusty attic. The pain was excruciating, an agonizing metamorphosis that pushed him to the very edge of endurance.

He cried out, a guttural, animalistic sound that was half scream, half roar, the raw, primal cry of a warrior being reborn. The air around him shimmered with an ethereal energy, a tangible manifestation of the Viking spirits merging with his own. He felt the phantom weight of armor, the familiar pressure of weapons against his skin – sensations that were not his own, yet utterly real. He felt the phantom itch of a beard against his jaw, a sensation he instinctively knew to be Bjorn's.

The changes were profound and complete. His height increased by several inches, his frame broadening to accommodate the immense strength that now coursed through his veins. His hands, once delicate and pale, became calloused and strong, his fingers thick and capable, each joint honed and strengthened by centuries of battle. His fingernails thickened and darkened, taking on the rough texture of polished horn. The muscles in his arms and shoulders bulged, his biceps and triceps practically bursting from his skin. His legs, once thin and wiry, transformed into pillars of raw power, capable of carrying the weight of a man twice his size. His posture straightened, his back no longer rounded with the weariness of his previous life but erect and powerful, the posture of a seasoned warrior, prepared for battle.

His senses sharpened dramatically. Sounds, once distant and muffled, became crisp and clear, sharp enough to discern individual voices in a crowded marketplace from a great distance. Scents, once faint and indistinguishable, flooded his awareness, his nose picking up the faint aroma of woodsmoke and salt from the distant ocean. His vision extended, taking in the intricate details of the attic's dusty woodwork, the faint scratches on the floorboards, even the minute particles of dust dancing in the faint light filtering through the grime-coated window. His sense of touch became hyper-sensitive; he could feel the texture of the rough wood under his hands, the subtle variations of temperature across his skin, even the microscopic ridges of the locket's ancient runes. His hearing was so acute, he could hear the faint chirp of crickets from the neighboring meadow, the rustling of leaves in the distant forest, the soft thud of his own heart beating against his ribs.

But the most profound transformation was not physical, but mental. The memories of the five Viking warriors flooded his mind, a torrent of sensations, emotions, and experiences. He experienced their victories, their triumphs, their intense joy in battle, but also their losses, their tragedies, and their heart-wrenching griefs. He felt their triumphs, tasting the victory of hard-fought battles, celebrating with them amidst joyous feasts and raucous songs. He felt their intense camaraderie, the strong bonds of loyalty and brotherhood that held them together in the face of death. He experienced their losses, the agonizing grief of comrades slain in battle, the crushing weight of defeat, the crushing horror of their final stand on that fog-shrouded island. He felt the chilling sting of death's cold embrace; not once, but five times. The memory of the blades slicing through flesh, the crushing weight of bodies falling, the raw and brutal agony of the dying - all these impressions were indelibly etched onto his consciousness.

It wasn't merely the observation of their lives, but the true and complete visceral experience of them. The smell of blood, the texture of cold steel, the bone-jarring impact of brutal blows, the taste of salty sea air mingled with the metallic tang of blood. These impressions were not just memories; they were like wounds reopening, scarring his mind as deeply as they had scarred their bodies. His mind struggled to process the onslaught of information, battling the conflicting realities of his own life, juxtaposed with the lives of warriors long dead.

The pain was more than just physical; it was an emotional maelstrom, a chaotic blend of conflicting sensations that threatened to overwhelm him. He felt the fierce pride and unwavering loyalty of

Bjorn, the relentless fury of Olaf, the stoic determination of Leif, and the synchronized precision of Ragnar and Harald. He felt their pain, their grief, their rage, their fear, as vividly as if he had lived their lives. His emotions shifted, often drastically, from moment to moment, sometimes feeling their exhilaration of victory, then suddenly succumbing to the despair of the massacre, as their individual memories would flash before his mind in vivid detail.

The transformations didn't happen all at once. There were periods of intense pain punctuated by brief respites, periods where the process would seemingly cease, only to resume with increased intensity. Each wave of transformation brought with it another layer of Viking memory and strength, another fragment of their personalities that merged with his own. The changes were not just physical; they altered his very essence, forging a new identity from the fusion of his own being with the ancient warriors. He was no longer simply Elias; he was Elias imbued with the strength, the skill, and the memories of five fallen Viking heroes. He was a vessel, a conduit, a living testament to the power of the past. His body was a testament to the struggle, a battleground where the present and the past fought for dominance.

He stumbled to his feet, his legs shaky but surprisingly strong. He looked down at his hands, their appearance starkly different from the soft, pale hands he remembered. They were rough and scarred, yet strong and capable, the calluses were a testament to years of wielding weapons, handling tools, and gripping shields in the face of impossible odds. He moved his arms, flexing the immense muscles beneath his skin, testing the newfound power. His body felt heavy, yet he also felt an almost supernatural lightness, the agility of a cat, a predatory grace he had never possessed before. He was no longer a frail outcast but a powerful warrior, ready to face whatever challenges lay ahead. The transformation was complete. He was ready. He was a Viking. He was more. He was their hope. And the fight was far from over.

The air crackled with an unseen energy, a palpable tension that hummed in the very bones of the old house. Elias, still reeling from the cataclysmic transformation, felt it as a prickling sensation on his skin, a warning sign that something was coming, something powerful and malevolent. He stood, his newly forged Viking strength a reassuring presence beneath his skin, but his mind raced, attempting to piece together the fragmented memories of the warriors, searching for any clue to the approaching threat.

The attic window, grimy and neglected, offered a fragmented view of the darkening landscape. He saw nothing unusual, just the familiar silhouettes of the distant hills and the swaying branches of the ancient oak trees that bordered his property. Yet, the feeling persisted, a premonition of impending doom, sharp and undeniable. It was then that he saw her.

A flicker of movement at the edge of his vision, a subtle shift in the shadows that escaped his initially heightened senses, but not the newly sharpened instincts of a thousand years of Viking battle experience. He turned slowly, his muscles coiled, ready to spring into action. At the edge of the overgrown garden, barely visible in the fading twilight, a figure emerged from the concealing shadows.

She was tall and slender, her movements fluid and graceful, like a wraith drifting on the wind. Her face was obscured by a deep cowl, but even from a distance, Elias could sense the raw power emanating from her, a chilling aura that sent a shiver down his spine. The air around her crackled and shimmered, and he sensed a potent magic, dark and ancient, that felt both terrifying and alluring. This was no ordinary woman; this was Morwen, the sorceress of legend.

As she moved closer, the details of her appearance slowly became apparent. Her features were striking, sharp and angular, her eyes gleaming with an unnatural light, eyes that seemed to pierce through him, searing his very soul. They were the eyes of a predator, filled with an ancient power and a chilling determination. Her hands, long and delicate, moved with a practiced grace, and he felt a visceral sense of dread; the very air seemed to vibrate with her potent magic. She was beautiful, in a disturbing, almost terrifying way, her beauty tainted by the dark power that emanated from her.

He felt a surge of fear, a primal instinct urging him to flee, to hide. But something deep within him, the indomitable spirit of the five Vikings, resisted. He stood his ground, his newly forged muscles tense, his senses honed to a razor's edge. This was not the weak, uncertain Elias he had been moments before. This was a warrior, forged in the fires of centuries of battle.

Morwen stopped a few feet away, her eyes fixed on him. The silence that followed was thick and heavy, charged with the unspoken tension between them. He sensed a recognition in her gaze, an understanding of the transformation he had undergone. She seemed to know exactly what he was, what he had become.

"The locket," she finally spoke, her voice a low, melodious whisper that carried a chilling undertone. Her words were laced with an ancient tongue, an echo of a forgotten era, yet somehow understandable. "Its power awakens. The spirits stir. I sensed it."

Elias remained silent, his eyes locked with hers, his new strength reassuring him, but the cold intensity of her gaze unsettled him. Her words confirmed his own suspicions. The visions, the transformation; it was all connected to her, to the locket, and now, to this terrifying confrontation.

"You have awakened them," Morwen continued, her voice gaining strength, a chilling certainty edging her tone. "Five souls, bound to that cursed amulet for centuries. Five warriors, reborn within a vessel unworthy of their power." Her eyes narrowed slightly, a hint of contempt crossing her features. "But their power is mine to claim."

Elias felt a surge of anger, a fierce protectiveness towards the Vikings whose memories now formed a part of him. He was their vessel, their protector, and he would not allow this sorceress to claim them, not now, not ever.

"You will not touch them," he growled, his voice raspy but powerful, bearing the rough timbre of a seasoned Viking. The words shocked even him; his voice was stronger, deeper, somehow more...ancient.

Morwen laughed, a low, guttural sound that echoed through the deserted attic, causing the old wood to creak and groan under the strain. "You dare defy me, little vessel? You, who are merely a conduit for their power? You think you can withstand my might?"

"I am more than a vessel," Elias retorted, his resolve hardening. "I am their heir, and I will defend their legacy."

Morwen's laughter ceased abruptly, replaced by a chilling silence that spoke volumes of her contempt. She raised a hand, and a faint green glow surrounded it, a tangible manifestation of her potent magic. The air thrummed with a potent energy, the very fabric of reality seeming to warp and distort around her. This was no ordinary sorcery; this was the power of centuries, the dark magic of a vengeful spirit, and it filled Elias with a chilling foreboding.

"Then prove it," Morwen hissed, her voice dripping with menace. "Prove that you can withstand the power of the ancient ones, the might of the blood moon, and the wrath of Morwen."

With a graceful yet menacing movement, she turned and vanished into the shadows, leaving Elias alone in the echoing stillness of the attic, the weight of her threat hanging heavy in the air. He knew this was only the beginning, the first act in a much larger, far more terrifying drama. The sorceress had declared her intentions, and the stage was set for a battle that would determine not only his fate, but the fate of the world itself. The fight to protect the souls of the five Viking warriors, and perhaps even more, had begun. The return of the sorceress was not a mere coincidence, it was the beginning of a war, a war for the very soul of the land. And Elias, the reluctant warrior, was at the very heart of it. He had to prepare, to gather his strength, both his own and that of the five Vikings he now carried within him. He had to find his allies, the outcasts who would join

him in this desperate fight against an overwhelming enemy. The blood moon ritual was fast approaching, and the time for decisive action was at hand.

The weight of Morwen's threat pressed down on Elias like a physical burden. The ancient oak trees outside his window seemed to groan under the strain, their branches swaying in a silent symphony of impending doom. He knew he couldn't face this alone. He needed allies, unlikely allies, people who, like him, were considered outcasts, outsiders, those who understood the sting of rejection and the strength found in defiance.

His first thought was Finn, a tech-savvy recluse who lived on the outskirts of town, a man shrouded in mystery, his workshop a labyrinth of wires, circuit boards, and forgotten technology. Finn had always been an enigma, a loner who preferred the company of machines to people. But Elias remembered Finn's quiet intensity, the sharp intelligence hidden behind a façade of indifference. He knew Finn possessed skills that could prove invaluable in their fight against Morwen. He could build weapons, analyze arcane symbols, even perhaps locate the sorceress's hidden lair using satellite imagery if he could be persuaded to cooperate. The challenge was to reach him, to convince him to abandon his self-imposed isolation and join a fight that seemed hopeless.

Leaving the old house, a sense of urgency propelled him through the night. The air was heavy with the scent of damp earth and impending rain. The moon, a sliver of silver in the inky sky, cast long shadows that danced and writhed like restless spirits. He reached Finn's dilapidated workshop, a ramshackle structure hidden amidst a tangle of overgrown vines and rusted machinery. He hesitated, remembering Finn's unpredictable nature, but the urgency of the situation pushed him forward.

He pounded on the heavy oak door, its surface scarred and worn. The sound echoed in the oppressive silence, then, after a moment that felt like an eternity, a gruff voice called out from within. "Who's there? And what do you want?"

Elias explained his situation, the locket, the sorceress, the imminent threat. He spoke of the five Vikings within him, their strength, their memories, their shared destiny. He painted a vivid picture of impending doom, a cataclysmic battle against overwhelming odds, a fight for the very survival of the kingdom. He spoke of Finn's unique skills, his potential to be a crucial part of their team. To his surprise, Finn listened patiently, his eyes, usually hidden behind thick lenses, fixed on Elias with an unusual intensity.

When Elias finished, Finn remained silent for a long moment, a strange contemplative stillness pervading his workshop. Then, a faint smile touched his lips. "You're looking for help," he stated, his voice surprisingly devoid of his usual gruffness. "And you've chosen me. Interesting."

The next ally he sought was Anya, a streetwise artist who lived in the city's underbelly, a world of shadows and secrets. Her vibrant graffiti adorned the city walls, a testament to her rebellious spirit and incredible talent. She possessed street smarts that no university could teach, a network of contacts spanning the city's underclass. More importantly, she possessed an uncanny ability to decipher symbolism and to identify hidden meanings in the chaos of urban life. Elias suspected that her skills could be crucial in interpreting ancient runes and deciphering Morwen's plans.

Finding Anya was easier than expected. She was known for her defiant spirit and bold creativity, traits that had both attracted her a dedicated following and drawn her into frequent clashes with the authorities. Elias found her amidst a crowd of onlookers, engrossed in painting a mural of a defiant phoenix rising from flames – a powerful metaphor, he thought, for their impending battle.

He approached her cautiously, aware that Anya was not known for her patience. He explained the situation as succinctly as possible, emphasizing the urgency, the danger, and Anya's unique contribution. He spoke of the ancient symbolism embedded in the fight against the sorceress, suggesting that her intuitive understanding of art and hidden meanings could be instrumental in their quest.

Anya listened intently, her sharp eyes never leaving Elias' face. When he finished, she let out a low whistle. "So, a Viking-possessed kid needs help from a street artist to take down a vengeful sorceress," she said, a smirk playing on her lips. "This is too good to be true. I'm in." Her acceptance was surprisingly straightforward, perhaps fueled by her inherent fascination with the extraordinary and her thirst for adventure.

Finally, Elias turned to the old historian, Professor Alistair, a man steeped in the lore and legends of the ancient kingdom, a keeper of forgotten histories and secrets. Alistair was a recluse who had dedicated his life to the study of the past, his knowledge unparalleled. Elias suspected that Alistair's understanding of Morwen's history, her motivations, and her rituals, could prove decisive in their fight.

Finding Alistair was not difficult. He inhabited a small, book-lined cottage on the university grounds, a sanctuary filled with the scent of old paper and forgotten times. Alistair was old, frail, his hands gnarled with age, but his mind was as sharp as ever, a vast library of historical knowledge ready to be tapped.

Elias found Alistair peacefully reading in his dimly lit study. He explained the situation, focusing on the historical significance of Morwen and the blood moon ritual. Alistair listened attentively, his eyes flickering with recognition. He had been aware of the legend, but had dismissed it as a mere superstition, something for children's stories. Now, it seemed, the legend had become horrifying reality.

Alistair, surprisingly, did not hesitate. He recognized the gravity of the situation, the looming threat to the kingdom, and his own responsibility to contribute his knowledge to the cause. The very weight of history itself propelled him to his feet.

With his unlikely allies gathered – the tech-savvy recluse, the streetwise artist, and the wise old historian – Elias felt a surge of confidence, a newfound strength that went beyond the Viking spirits within him. He was not merely a vessel, he was a leader, a commander gathering his forces in preparation for a war that would determine the fate of the world. He was no longer just Elias; he was Elias, son of the Vikings, leader of the outcasts, protector of the kingdom. The blood moon ritual drew ever closer, but he was ready, his alliances forged, his strategy forming, and his determination unwavering. The fight had begun.

The locket pulsed against Elias's chest, a warm, insistent thrumming that resonated deep within his bones. He hadn't anticipated the intensity of the experience, the sheer tidal wave of memory that crashed over him, shattering the fragile peace he'd found in assembling his unlikely alliance. It wasn't just a glimpse into the past, it was a complete immersion, a visceral reliving of another life, another time. The world around him faded, replaced by a biting wind and the salty tang of the sea.

He *was* Bjorn.

The roar of the waves was deafening, a constant, relentless percussion against the jagged rocks of the island. The air hung heavy with the smell of brine and woodsmoke, a stark contrast to the sterile scent of antiseptic that had clung to him for so long in the sterile confines of the orphanage. He saw himself, a young man, his hair the color of raven's wings, his eyes the piercing blue of a winter sky. He was strong, impossibly strong, his muscles rippling beneath his roughspun tunic. He commanded a longship, its dragon-head prow slicing through the churning water. His men, his brothers-in-arms, were with him, their faces etched with the same fierce loyalty and grim determination that mirrored his own.

The memory unfolded in a series of vivid snapshots: the thrill of the raid, the clash of steel, the triumphant cries of victory. He felt the weight of his axe, the satisfying heft of it in his hands, the spray of blood as it cleaved through the enemy's shields. He was a warrior, a leader, a man of legend in his own time. He felt the fierce pride that swelled in his chest, the unwavering belief in his own invincibility. This was Bjorn, son of Ragnar, the terror of the northern seas, the scourge of the coastlines, the unflinching defender of his people.

But the vibrant tapestry of victory was soon woven with threads of darkness. The memories shifted, the exhilarating rush of battle replaced by a chilling sense of foreboding. The laughter of his comrades faded into hushed whispers, replaced by the chilling silence that precedes a storm. He saw the fog rolling in, a dense, unnatural blanket that shrouded the island in an eerie stillness. It wasn't the natural fog that accompanied storm; it seemed to emanate from a darker force, something ancient and malevolent. This time, it wasn't the thrill of battle; it was the terror of the unknown.

The next scene was a massacre. A brutal, merciless slaughter. The screams of his men still echoed in Elias's ears long after the memory faded. Bjorn fought with the ferocity of a cornered wolf, but he was outnumbered, outmatched. He saw his comrades fall one by one, their blood staining the rocky shore, their lives extinguished like flickering flames. He saw the sorceress, Morwen, her face a mask of cruel triumph, her eyes burning with an unnatural fire. Her magic was a tangible force, a swirling vortex of dark energy that twisted the very fabric of reality.

The agony of those final moments was almost unbearable. Bjorn fought with a desperate courage, his axe a blur of motion, but it was no use. He felt the searing pain of the sorceress's magic, a burning that consumed him from the inside out. He saw the faces of his fallen brothers, their eyes reflecting his own despair. He saw his own wife and children, their faces filled with a primal fear that mirrored his own. The memory of his wife's fear was a sharp physical pain, a dagger in his heart.

The final image was a blur of chaos and despair; the sorceress's triumphant laughter ringing in his ears, the agonizing sensation of his life force being ripped away, his soul trapped, the taste of blood and salt mingling on his tongue. Then, darkness. A suffocating, unending darkness.

The visions ended abruptly, leaving Elias gasping for breath, his body drenched in a cold sweat. The weight of Bjorn's memories settled upon him, a crushing burden of loss and sorrow. He was no longer just Elias, the outcast; he was also Bjorn, the warrior, the leader, the victim. The experiences were his, yet they were not his.

He carried the weight of a thousand years of Viking history, of triumphs and tragedies, of love and loss. The memories weren't just about battle and death. They revealed a man of surprising depth. He saw Bjorn's tender moments: his quiet laughter with his wife, the playful wrestling matches with his children, his fierce protectiveness over his family. He learned about Bjorn's deep loyalty to his men, his unwavering commitment to their well-being. He witnessed the agonizing grief that consumed Bjorn as he watched his comrades perish. The sorrow he felt was a chilling echo of his own loneliness. It was a sorrow that resonated with the aching emptiness that had always been a part of Elias's own life. He understood Bjorn's struggles, his regrets, his unwavering love, his ultimate sacrifice.

He discovered the complexity of Bjorn's character, the flaws that balanced his undeniable strength. He was not a flawless hero, a mythical legend. He was a man, burdened by the weight of responsibility, haunted by the specter of his own mortality, a man who loved fiercely and lost tragically. The burden of his regrets was almost as heavy as the weight of the battleaxe he wielded.

Bjorn's past wasn't just a historical narrative; it was a personal revelation, a profound insight into the heart of a warrior. It was a story of courage and sacrifice, of loyalty and loss, of love and despair. It was a story that resonated deeply with Elias, adding another layer of complexity to his own identity, his own journey. It was a burden, certainly, but also a source of profound strength.

The locket pulsed again, a rhythmic reminder of the power it held, the legacy it carried. Elias felt a surge of determination, a resolve hardened by Bjorn's memories, by his pain, by his ultimate sacrifice. He wouldn't let Bjorn's death be in vain. He wouldn't let Morwen succeed. He wouldn't let the darkness consume the kingdom. He had allies now, unlikely allies, forged in the crucible of desperation and the shared understanding of being outcast. Together, they would face Morwen, together they would confront the darkness, and together they would fight for the future. The blood moon was near, but he was ready. He was Bjorn. He was Elias. And he would not fail. The weight of five thousand years of Viking spirit rested on his shoulders, and he would bear it. He would fight. He would win. For Bjorn. For his allies. For the kingdom. For himself.

Chapter 7: Understanding the Curse

The locket's thrumming intensified, a rhythmic pulse mirroring the frantic beat of Elias's heart. Bjorn's memories, initially a chaotic torrent, began to coalesce, revealing a clearer picture of the events leading up to the massacre. The fog, he realized, wasn't simply a weather phenomenon; it was a tangible manifestation of Morwen's magic, a suffocating shroud that warped perception and amplified fear. It was a veil of darkness that not only obscured the island but also obscured the truth, twisting the minds of its victims.

He saw fleeting glimpses of Morwen's rituals, bizarre ceremonies performed under the malevolent glow of the blood moon. The air crackled with dark energy, the very ground seeming to writhe beneath her feet. He saw symbols etched into the rocks, runes of an ancient, forgotten language, pulsating with an ominous power. These weren't merely decorative carvings; they were conduits of Morwen's magic, feeding her power and amplifying her influence.

The curse wasn't simply a matter of trapping the Vikings' souls; it was a far more intricate and sinister design. Morwen hadn't merely imprisoned them; she had bound their life force to her own malevolent will. Their very essence was intertwined with the demonic entity she sought to resurrect – a being whose name was whispered only in hushed tones, a being whose power was described in terrified legends. Bjorn's memories revealed fragments of their conversations, hushed warnings from elders about the return of this ancient entity, a chilling reminder that their struggle was about far more than just their own survival. It was about the survival of their people, the fate of the kingdom itself.

The demon warlord, whose name Elias could not quite grasp, was a being of immense power, capable of shattering kingdoms and reshaping reality. Morwen's plan wasn't merely to resurrect him; it was to utilize the bound spirits of the Vikings to amplify his power, to ensure his resurgence was not a mere awakening but a cataclysmic eruption of dark energy that would engulf the world in eternal night.

The Vikings' strength, their battle-hardened souls, were the fuel that would ignite Morwen's horrifying ritual. Each Viking's soul contributed to this terrifying ritual. Elias carried not just the memories and strength of one, but five warriors; their combined power made him a critical component in Morwen's scheme – a terrifying and dangerous realization.

The images shifted, revealing fragments of a conversation between Morwen and one of her followers, a hulking brute with eyes like chips of obsidian. They spoke of the ritual, of the blood moon's alignment with the ancient runes, of the precise moment when the warlord's power would be unleashed. Morwen's words dripped with an unsettling confidence, her voice a chilling blend of power and chilling arrogance. The certainty in her voice sent a shiver down Elias's spine. This was not simply a desperate gamble; it was a carefully orchestrated plan, centuries in the making.

The details were often fragmented, obscured by the chaotic surge of Bjorn's dying moments, yet the overall picture began to emerge with chilling clarity. The curse wasn't just about death; it was about control, about manipulating the life force of the fallen warriors to fuel Morwen's dark ambition. It was a parasitic bond, feeding Morwen's power and draining the Vikings of their very essence. The souls of the Vikings were not simply trapped; they were bound to her will, bound to the summoning of the demon warlord. The more she drew from them, the more powerful she became, the closer she came to unleashing the full horror of her plan.

He understood now the terrifying weight of the responsibility that rested upon his shoulders. He wasn't merely carrying the memories and strength of five fallen warriors; he was carrying their hopes, their dreams, their unfinished business. He was the vessel through which Morwen sought to unleash a darkness that could consume the world.

Elias felt a surge of icy dread. The implications of Morwen's plan were devastating; the destruction she sought was on a scale he could scarcely comprehend. But within that dread, a spark of defiance ignited. He wouldn't let her succeed. He wouldn't let Bjorn, or any of the other fallen warriors, die in vain. Their sacrifice would not be meaningless. He would use their strength, their memories, their will, to stop her, even if it meant facing unimaginable horrors.

The weight of five thousand years, or perhaps more, pressed down upon him; the combined weight of their lives, their deaths, their unfulfilled destinies, their hopes and dreams. The knowledge that their very spirits were entwined with his gave him both an incredible power, and a crushing burden. It was a weight that threatened to break him, but also a weight that fueled his resolve. He would carry their spirits, their fight, their struggle for survival, for justice, for hope.

Understanding the nature of the curse offered Elias a new perspective. He realized that defeating Morwen wasn't just a matter of brute strength; it required a deep understanding of her magic, of the intricate web of dark energy she had woven. He needed to find a way to sever the bonds that connected the Vikings' souls to her, to break the parasitic link that fueled her power. But how? The answer was elusive, yet the determination to find it burned fiercely within him.

The memories continued to flow, offering glimpses of Morwen's rituals, her incantations, the symbols she used. He saw fragments of ancient texts, cryptic writings that hinted at the origins of her power, the source of the demon warlord's strength. The runes, he realized, were more than just symbols; they were keys, unlocking the ancient magic that Morwen wielded, keys that might also hold the answer to breaking her control. This insight was not only intellectual but also deeply intuitive, resonating with the locket's rhythmic beat.

The next few days were a blur of frantic activity. Elias, guided by the Vikings' fragmented memories, delved into ancient texts, obscure historical records, and forgotten legends. He poured over dusty tomes in forgotten libraries, seeking clues, any shred of information that might offer a path to victory. He worked tirelessly, driven by a desperate need to understand the enemy, to find a weakness in Morwen's seemingly impenetrable defenses. His allies, initially skeptical, watched with a growing sense of awe and respect as they witnessed Elias's transformation, his growing understanding of the ancient magic and its intricate workings.

Their support wasn't merely practical; it was emotional, a lifeline in the face of overwhelming odds. They understood what he was doing, what he was fighting for; they were fighting alongside him, not merely as allies, but as brothers, united by a shared purpose. Their initial fear and skepticism had evolved into a determination born of shared understanding and faith in Elias. He was no longer merely an outcast; he was their leader, the one who held the key to their survival, to the survival of the kingdom.

The blood moon loomed closer, its crimson glow painting the night sky in a horrifying spectacle. Time was running out, but Elias was prepared. He had pieced together the clues, deciphered the runes, and unearthed the hidden knowledge needed to confront Morwen.

The final battle was fast approaching; a battle not only for their lives but for the fate of the world. The combined knowledge of five Vikings, their individual experiences, and the weight of their combined spirits resting on him gave Elias an unusual power. He was ready. He was Bjorn. He was Harald. He was Leif. He was Ragnar. He was Olaf. And he was Elias. And he would not fail.

The weight of five Viking souls settled upon Elias, a burden both crushing and exhilarating. He felt their strength surge through him, a raw power that hummed beneath his skin, yet the memories they imparted weren't just of glorious battle; they were of brutal lessons learned in the harsh crucible of war. They showed him strategies, tactics, and the brutal realities of combat—a stark contrast to the historical accounts he had previously read.

Their training began not in a grand hall or martial arts dojo, but in the shadowed depths of an abandoned quarry. The air hung heavy with the scent of damp earth and decay, a fitting backdrop for the brutal reality of their preparation. Guided by the spectral forms of Bjorn, Harald, Leif, Ragnar, and Olaf, Elias and his friends, a ragtag band of outcasts united by their shared cause, embarked on a rigorous regimen designed to push them beyond the limits of their endurance.

Bjorn, the fiercest of the five, focused on hand-to-hand combat, teaching them the brutal efficiency of Viking fighting styles. His instruction was as relentless as a winter storm, each blow a lesson in survival. He drilled them relentlessly, demanding precision, speed, and unwavering focus. They sparred until their muscles screamed in protest, their bodies aching with a fatigue they'd never experienced before. He taught them to fight not merely with strength, but with cunning, to anticipate their opponent's movements, to exploit their weaknesses, and to strike with deadly precision. He hammered home the importance of adaptability, showing them how to shift between various fighting stances, adapting to different opponents and unforeseen circumstances.

Harald, a master strategist, taught them the art of warfare. He didn't focus solely on individual combat, but on the coordinated movements of a group, the importance of teamwork and cohesion. He explained siege warfare, open battle tactics, and even the intricacies of guerilla warfare, emphasizing the need to understand the battlefield, to utilize the terrain to their advantage, and to anticipate their opponent's moves before they were even made. He stressed the importance of communication, of clear signals and quick responses – crucial elements in the chaotic maelstrom of battle.

Leif, a master swordsman, refined their technique with his legendary skill. He taught them different sword fighting styles, from the powerful two-handed swings of the great axe to the lightning-fast precision of the single-handed sword. He emphasized the importance of balance, control, and the understanding of the weapon's weight, showing them how to use their bodies as an extension of the blade. He meticulously corrected their stances, their footwork, and the trajectory of their strikes, molding their movements into an art form honed to deadly perfection.

Ragnar, a seasoned archer, taught them the art of ranged combat. He showed them how to gauge distance, judge wind speed, and anticipate their target's movements, all while maintaining a steady aim. He pushed them to their limits, challenging their physical endurance and their mental fortitude, urging them to hone their skills until their shots were as deadly as any warrior's blade. He didn't just teach them archery; he taught them patience, observation, and strategic thinking, essential skills for any soldier.

Olaf, a skilled sailor and navigator, provided a different kind of training. He taught them to read the currents, understand the winds, and navigate unfamiliar waters. His training wasn't about brute force, but about adaptability and resourcefulness, skills that would prove invaluable during their quest to confront Morwen. He taught them survival techniques, how to find food and shelter in the wilderness, and how to utilize the natural environment to their advantage. He made them realize that even the smallest detail could mean life or death.

Their training was far more than simply mastering weapons; it was about honing their minds as well as their bodies. They learned to control their fear, to conquer their doubts, and to tap into the reserves of strength they never knew they possessed. Elias learned how to channel the power of the five Vikings, to merge their individual skills into a unified force, creating a synergy that amplified their abilities far beyond what any of them could achieve alone. The Vikings' spirits guided them, pushing them to their limits, honing their skills until they moved as one, a perfectly coordinated unit, a force to be reckoned with.

The training was brutal, relentless, pushing them to the very edge of their physical and mental capabilities. There were times when they faltered, when doubt threatened to consume them, when the weight of their task seemed insurmountable. But they persevered, spurred on by Elias's unwavering determination and the spectral encouragement of the fallen warriors. They learned to rely on each other, to trust in their comrades, and to support each other through the darkest moments of their arduous preparation. Their bond deepened, forged in the fires of adversity, becoming as strong and unbreakable as the ancient weapons they wielded.

As the blood moon approached, the final stage of their training intensified. It was no longer about perfecting individual skills, but about integrating those skills into a unified strategy, about mastering the art of coordinated warfare. They practiced intricate battle formations, rehearsing different scenarios, anticipating every possible contingency. They learned to anticipate Morwen's tactics, utilizing the Vikings' collective knowledge to counteract her dark magic.

They practiced fighting in the shadows, utilizing the terrain to their advantage, mimicking the fog-shrouded island where the Vikings had met their fate. They learned to fight not only against flesh and blood, but against illusions and dark magic, preparing for the mind-bending tactics Morwen would undoubtedly unleash. They used their combined knowledge of history, magic, and mythology to strategize, to anticipate Morwen's every move.

The most difficult part of their training, however, involved learning to harness and control Elias's abilities. The five spirits within him were powerful, but also volatile. Elias had to learn how to channel their power, to summon their individual strengths at will, without allowing their conflicting personalities to overwhelm him. This required immense mental discipline, a feat made all the more challenging by the looming threat of the blood moon ritual.

Days bled into nights, and nights were consumed by relentless training. They pushed their bodies to the very brink of exhaustion, their minds stretched taut with worry and fear, but their bond remained unshaken. They were no longer just a group of outcasts; they were a team, a family, a force united in their common purpose.

Finally, the day arrived when their training culminated in a final, grueling test. They faced a simulated battle, a recreation of the massacre on the fog-shrouded island, complete with illusions, traps, and formidable opponents meant to replicate Morwen's formidable forces. The simulation was brutal, pushing them to the limits of their endurance, but they persevered, using their combined skills and unwavering determination to overcome every obstacle. The victory was hard-won, but it cemented their readiness for the coming confrontation. They had honed their skills, they had sharpened their strategies, they had forged an unbreakable bond, and they were ready to face Morwen and her demonic army.

The blood moon hung heavy in the sky, a malevolent eye watching their preparations. Time was running out. Yet, Elias and his friends stood ready, their hearts filled with a mixture of fear and determination. They were ready to face their destiny, to confront the horrors that awaited them, and to fight for the survival of the world. The whispers of the past had guided them, and the lessons they learned in training would dictate their fate in the fight to come. The battle for the kingdom, and perhaps the world, was about to begin.

Chapter 9: The Prophecy

The air in the abandoned church crackled with an unseen energy, a palpable tension that hung heavier than the dust motes dancing in the slivers of moonlight piercing the shattered stained-glass windows. Elias, his senses heightened by the Viking souls within him, felt it first – a tremor in the very fabric of reality, a whisper carried on the wind. It wasn't the wind itself, but something far older, far deeper; the echo of a forgotten power stirring from its slumber.

He traced a finger along the cold, worn surface of the locket, its intricate carvings pulsing faintly beneath his touch. Inside, the five Viking spirits swirled, a maelstrom of raw power and ancient memories. Bjorn, his eyes blazing with a fierce intensity even in death, nudged Elias's mind, urging him forward. "The prophecy," he whispered, the words echoing in Elias's mind, "it speaks of you."

Harald, ever the strategist, projected images into Elias's mind – fragmented visions of a future both glorious and terrifying: a world plunged into darkness, the earth stained crimson with blood, and then, a single figure standing defiant amidst the chaos, wielding a weapon of unimaginable power. The figure was... Elias.

Leif, his spectral form shimmering, presented Elias with a scroll, ancient and brittle, its script penned in a language long lost to time. It was the prophecy, a cryptic poem of immense power and chilling implications, filled with riddles and veiled metaphors. Each line was a puzzle, each word heavy with symbolic meaning. The language was complex, but the images that accompanied them were vivid and chilling, painting a horrifying picture of the oncoming war.

Ragnar, his bow taut in his spectral hand, focused Elias' attention on a particular passage. It spoke of a "blood moon's embrace," a time when the veil between worlds thinned, allowing the dark forces to spill into the mortal realm. It spoke of a "demon warlord," Morwen's master, a being of immense power whose name sent shivers down their collective spines. The prophecy detailed the warlord's rise, his reign of terror, and the unimaginable destruction he would unleash.

Olaf, his sea-worn eyes filled with an ancient wisdom, provided the historical context. He pointed to passages that referenced events long past, connecting the prophecy to the events that led to the Vikings' demise. It was a cyclical narrative, a tapestry woven from the threads of time, each event influencing the next, creating a chain reaction that culminated in the present. The prophecy indicated that the warlord's return was tied inextricably to Morwen's actions, a chilling realization that sent a wave of dread through their spectral ranks.

The prophecy revealed a deeper truth: Elias wasn't just a vessel for the Viking souls; he was the key to fulfilling it. He was the "chosen one," the prophesied hero who would stand against the demon warlord and save the world from impending doom. It was a destiny he never sought, a burden thrust upon him against his will. The images showed him defeating the warlord, a powerful figure wielding a mystical weapon forged from the souls of the Vikings themselves.

The prophecy was riddled with symbolism. The blood moon represented not just a celestial event but a time of spiritual vulnerability, a gateway for the demonic forces. The "fog-shrouded island" served as a metaphorical representation of the world succumbing to despair. The "five souls united" symbolized the power Elias had inherited, the strength of their collective spirits forming a weapon against the darkness. The cryptic verse spoke of a"weapon forged in fire," a "storm of steel," and a "shield of starlight." Each phrase echoed with hidden meanings that demanded further investigation.

The Viking spirits debated the interpretation, their spectral forms flickering with intensity as they pored over the ancient words. Bjorn, ever the warrior, focused on the direct, visceral imagery, emphasizing the battles to come and the strength they would need to prevail. Harald, in his usual thoughtful manner, dissected the strategic implications, highlighting the importance of planning and coordination. Leif analyzed the technical aspects, connecting the symbolic weaponry to tangible items and possibilities. Ragnar, ever the watchful guardian, interpreted the celestial alignments, tying the prophecy to the blood moon's return. Olaf, the seasoned sailor, brought the context of seafaring to the interpretation, recognizing metaphors linked to the ocean's treacherous currents.

Days turned into nights as they meticulously deciphered the prophecy. Each verse brought forth new questions, each answer spawned additional riddles. The cryptic language was a challenge, and the cryptic metaphors added another layer of complexity. They worked tirelessly, deciphering each line, searching for clues and hidden meanings. The passage that spoke of the "weapon forged in fire" proved especially problematic. Was it a literal weapon, or a symbolic representation of Elias's inner strength, forged in the crucible of their training?

As they unravelled the meaning, a chilling revelation emerged: the prophecy wasn't just a forecast; it was a guide. It described not only the impending doom but also the steps Elias must take to prevent it. It detailed a series of trials he had to face, each one a necessary step on his path to confronting the demon warlord. These trials involved mystical creatures, forgotten locations and hidden truths—a path fraught with danger. It revealed the location of hidden allies and resources, allies they would need to face the looming threat.

The more they studied the prophecy, the more they realized the depth of its wisdom and complexity. The weight of this destiny, this burden of fulfilling this ancient prophecy, pressed down on Elias. The prophecy was not just a simple prediction of the future; it was a complex and interconnected narrative that entwined past, present and future. It described not only Elias's journey but also the actions of Morwen and her master. The prophecy described Morwen's plan in detail, her rituals, and her methods to summon the demon warlord. This understanding gave them a crucial advantage, allowing them to anticipate Morwen's next moves.

Elias felt the weight of the world on his shoulders. He was no longer just a boy haunted by visions; he was the prophesied hero, the last hope against the forces of darkness. The responsibility was immense, the challenges seemingly insurmountable. Yet, something shifted within him. The fear was still there, a cold knot in his stomach, but it was overshadowed by a burgeoning sense of purpose, a fierce determination to fulfill the prophecy, to save the world that fate had thrust upon him.

The blood moon loomed closer, its ominous glow painting the sky in shades of crimson and dread. But Elias, guided by the whispers of the past and armed with the knowledge of the prophecy, felt a surge of strength he hadn't known before. He was ready. The training was complete, the prophecy understood. The final battle was about to begin. The fate of the kingdom, and indeed, the world, rested on his shoulders. The whispers of the past had led him here, and now, he would face his destiny.

The abandoned church, their sanctuary for days, felt suddenly claustrophobic. The air, once thick with the weight of prophecy, now vibrated with a different kind of energy – a palpable sense of impending conflict. Elias, Bjorn, Harald, Leif, Ragnar, and Olaf stood poised, their spectral forms shimmering faintly in the dim light. The whispers of the past had prepared them, but nothing could truly prepare them for the reality of facing Morwen's forces.

The first sign was a low growl, a guttural sound that seemed to rise from the very earth beneath their feet. It was followed by a chorus of similar growls, echoing and multiplying, creating a cacophony that sent shivers down Elias's spine. Then, they emerged from the shadows – grotesque creatures, twisted parodies of nature, their forms vaguely canine but with features that defied description.

Their eyes glowed with an unnatural luminescence, their claws dripping with a viscous, black ichor. They were Morwen's hounds, monstrous creatures forged from dark magic and shadow.

Bjorn, ever the warrior, was the first to react. "They are faster than we anticipated," he warned, his voice echoing in Elias's mind. "Their senses are heightened; they can smell our magic."

Harald, already formulating a strategy, barked orders. "Leif, Ragnar, create a diversion. Olaf, create a defensive perimeter. Elias and I will hold the center. We need to buy ourselves time."

The battle was brutal, a chaotic dance of shadow and steel. Leif's spectral spear, shimmering with ethereal energy, sliced through the air, leaving trails of crackling light. Ragnar's spectral arrows, tipped with solidified shadow, found their marks with unnerving accuracy. Olaf, using his knowledge of tides and currents, subtly manipulated the earth, creating pockets of instability that tripped and disoriented the hounds. However, their numbers were overwhelming, their attacks relentless.

Elias, empowered by the five Viking souls, fought with a ferocity he never knew he possessed. He moved with a speed and agility he couldn't have imagined just weeks prior. His strikes, guided by Bjorn's brutal instinct and Harald's tactical prowess, found their targets with deadly precision. He wielded a makeshift weapon – a sturdy branch from a fallen tree, reinforced with the remnants of a rusted iron fence, its surface now strangely resonating with a faint, magical glow. The prophecy's words of a "weapon forged in fire"seemed to find a literal echo in this crude, yet effective, implement.

Yet, even with their combined strength and skill, they were struggling. The hounds were relentless, their attacks relentless. Their numbers seemed endless, their ferocity unending. Elias felt the familiar pang of fear, the instinctive response to overwhelming odds, but the Vikings' spirits pushed back against it, reinforcing his resolve. He drew strength not only from their power but from their shared experiences, their shared memories of countless battles fought and won.

One by one, the hounds fell, their spectral forms dissolving into harmless mist as they were struck by the combined might of the Vikings and Elias. But for every one that fell, two more seemed to take its place. The battle was a test of endurance, a relentless onslaught that pushed them to their absolute limits. The air grew heavy with the smell of blood, both real and spectral, a grim testament to the brutal reality of their fight for survival.

Harald, his spectral form growing fainter, suffered a significant blow. One of the hounds, larger and more vicious than the others, had managed to land a devastating blow, tearing a hole in his spectral form. Elias saw Harald's energy begin to falter. The strategist, so calm and collected throughout the battle, was now in need of support.

Elias felt the desperate plea for aid emanating from Harald. This was not a theoretical battle, it was a fight for their very survival. Fear threatened to consume them again, but in that moment, Elias felt a rush of adrenaline unlike anything he had ever experienced. This was not just a battle between their forces and Morwen's, this was a fight for the souls of those who relied on them, a fight against the return of a demonic warlord that would consume the kingdom.

He pushed himself harder, fighting with a primal fury that shocked even himself. He channeled the rage of Bjorn, the cunning of Harald, the precision of Leif, the vigilance of Ragnar, and the wisdom of Olaf. Every blow was more precise, more powerful, filled with the weight of centuries of experience.

The battle raged on, a bloody and chaotic dance of death. The church, once a place of solace, was now a battlefield, its hallowed grounds stained crimson with spectral blood. As the final hound fell, a silent exhaustion descended upon them. They had won this battle, but the victory felt hollow, a fragile respite in a war that had only just begun.

The aftermath was grim. Harald's form was severely weakened, the damage from the hound's attack far more extensive than they'd first realized. He needed rest and healing. Elias, despite his own exhaustion, felt a sense of grim determination settle within him. This was just the first encounter. Morwen's forces were far greater, far more powerful, than they had anticipated. The prophecy's grim details were now a brutal reality.

The experience had been a profound awakening. They had faced their fears, confronted their limitations, and emerged victorious –but just barely. The battle had stripped away their illusions of invincibility, replacing them with a sobering understanding of the challenges that lay ahead. They had a taste of what was to come, and it tasted like bitter ash. The coming battles would not be as merciful. This first fight had taught them a vital lesson: survival demanded more than just strength; it demanded unity, strategy, and an unwavering resolve in the face of overwhelming odds. The blood moon's embrace was approaching, and with it, a far greater and more terrifying conflict. They had a brief respite, but the whispers of the past had given them a glimpse of their destiny, and now they braced themselves for the inevitable – a war that would determine the fate of the world. The fight had only just begun.

The battered remains of the church offered little comfort as they prepared for the next stage of their perilous journey. Harald, his spectral form still flickering weakly, leaned heavily against a crumbling stone pillar, his ethereal breath misting in the cold morning air. The battle had left its mark, not only on their physical forms but on their spirits as well. The relentless onslaught of Morwen's hounds had revealed the true scale of the threat they faced; a threat that extended far beyond the walls of the abandoned sanctuary.

"The island..." Harald rasped, his voice barely a whisper, "it lies shrouded in perpetual mist, they say. A place where the veil between worlds is thin, where the shadows themselves take form."

Elias, his own body aching from the exertion of battle, nodded grimly. The visions that had plagued him since discovering the locket had painted a vivid, terrifying picture of the island. He saw the massacre, a brutal slaughter under a blood-red moon, the Vikings falling one by one to the sorceress's dark magic. The images burned themselves into his mind, a constant reminder of the task that lay ahead. He felt the weight of their collective destiny, the fate of the kingdom resting on his young, albeit magically-enhanced shoulders.

Professor Alistair remained slightly apart from the group, hunched over a cracked tablet etched with faded runes. He scribbled in his journal with fevered precision, pausing only to glance toward Elias now and then, muttering comparisons between the locket's glow and a celestial diagram he'd once studied in the archives. "The runic alignment... it's accelerating," he murmured. "We may have less time than we thought."

Ragnar, ever vigilant, scanned their surroundings. "We must travel swiftly," he declared, his voice low and urgent. "Morwen will not wait for us to arrive. The blood moon is approaching. Time is our most precious enemy."

The journey began under a sky choked with heavy, grey clouds. The landscape, once familiar, now appeared menacing and foreboding. Twisted trees clawed at the sky, their branches gnarled and skeletal, like the fingers of grasping ghosts. The path ahead was treacherous, a narrow track that wound its way through a dense, impenetrable forest. The air grew colder, the damp chill seeping into their bones, even into Elias's magically-enhanced form.

As they delved deeper into the forest's embrace, the silence became unnerving, broken only by the crunch of their boots on the muddy path and the occasional snap of a twig underfoot. The oppressive atmosphere hung heavy upon them, a palpable sense of unease that unsettled even the seasoned warriors.

Then, they encountered the first of the island's guardians. These were not the monstrous hounds of Morwen's army, but something far more ancient, far more terrifying. Creatures of myth and legend, half-beast, half-shadow, their forms shifting and blurring at the edges of perception. Their eyes glowed with an eerie, internal light, and their movements were fluid and unpredictable, like the shifting mists that surrounded them.

The encounter was a harrowing test of their skills and their unity. Bjorn's raw strength, fueled by his Viking fury, was matched by Harald's tactical brilliance, and Leif and Ragnar's combined offensive power proved surprisingly effective against the ethereal nature of these creatures. Olaf, despite his frail spectral nature, used his earth magic to create traps and obstacles, disorienting the creatures and buying them precious time.

Elias, meanwhile, found himself fighting not only with the strength of the Vikings but with their accumulated wisdom. He learned to anticipate the creatures' attacks, to react with the speed and precision of a seasoned warrior, even as he felt the physical and emotional strain of wielding such immense power. The bond between them, forged in the crucible of battle, proved to be their greatest weapon.

Their combined effort proved a match for the shadowy creatures. As they fell, their forms dissipating into swirling mist, a sense of exhaustion settled upon them, but this encounter proved to be more than just a physical challenge. It was a test of their alliance, their mutual trust. They found renewed strength in their unity, understanding more deeply than before their collective dependence on each other.

The journey continued, each step forward a battle against the elements and the island's sinister guardians. They navigated treacherous bogs where the earth seemed to swallow them whole, scaled cliffs that scraped against the sky, and crossed raging rivers whose currents threatened to sweep them away. The physical toll was immense, their bodies weary, their spirits tested to their limits. Yet, they persevered. The visions of the massacre, the prophecies of impending doom, fueled their determination. They knew that failure was not an option.

The island's landscape was a reflection of its dark history. The twisted trees, the treacherous terrain, the ethereal guardians – all served as a constant reminder of the horrors that awaited them. The island itself seemed to breathe a malevolent energy, an oppressive weight that pressed down on them, threatening to crush their spirits.

Yet, even as they faced these challenges, Elias found a growing connection with the Vikings. Their memories, their experiences, their emotions – all flowed into him, enriching his understanding of their lives, their deaths, and their ongoing struggle. He felt their rage, their sorrow, their undying loyalty to each other. He saw their world, their battles, their victories, and their ultimate defeat at the hands of Morwen's power.

This connection brought with it not only strength but also a deep sense of responsibility. He was no longer just Elias, the outcast boy. He was the vessel for the souls of five Viking warriors, bound to a destiny that would determine the fate of the kingdom, perhaps even the world.

As they pushed forward, the mist grew thicker, more oppressive. The island's sinister heart lay just ahead, and the air crackled with a palpable sense of anticipation. The blood moon was rising, casting an eerie, crimson glow on the landscape, foreshadowing the final confrontation. Their journey was far from over, but they stood on the precipice of their destiny, ready to face the sorceress and her demonic forces in a climactic battle that would decide the fate of all they held dear. The island of shadows awaited, its dark secrets ready to be revealed.

The mist clung to them like a shroud, a damp, chilling embrace that seeped into their bones despite the growing intensity of the blood moon's crimson glow. The island, once a menacing presence, now felt actively hostile, its very air thick with an ancient, malevolent energy. They pressed onward, the spectral forms of the Vikings flickering faintly in the dim light, their ethereal bodies struggling against the island's oppressive power. Ragnar, ever the strategist, led the way, his keen eyes scanning the treacherous terrain.

Their progress was slow, agonizingly so. The path, barely discernible beneath the clinging mist, wound its way through a labyrinth of twisted trees and gnarled roots. The forest floor was a treacherous bog, its muddy surface yielding beneath their weight, threatening to swallow them whole. Each step was a battle against the elements, a constant struggle against the island's insidious grip.

It was Bjorn, his physical strength amplified by the locket's power, who first spotted the anomaly. A subtle shift in the mist, a faint glimmer of light through the dense foliage. He pointed, a guttural growl escaping his lips, a sound that echoed with the raw energy of a warrior roused from centuries of slumber.

"A ruin," Harald whispered, his voice barely audible above the whispering wind. "An ancient structure, hidden beneath the mist."

As they approached, the mist parted slightly, revealing a crumbling stone structure half-buried in the earth. It was a small, circular building, its stone walls weathered and worn, overgrown with moss and lichen. The entrance, barely visible, was arched and overgrown, leading into a darkness that seemed to swallow the remaining light.

Ragnar approached cautiously, his hand resting on the hilt of his spectral sword. He felt a shiver run down his spine, a premonition of the unseen dangers lurking within. "Caution," he warned, his voice low and urgent. "This place...it feels wrong. Ancient, yes, but tainted by something...dark."

Elias, guided by the Vikings' collective memory, felt a pull towards the structure, a sense of recognition, a whisper of forgotten knowledge resonating within his soul. It was as if the stones themselves were calling to him, urging him to uncover the secrets they held.

The entrance was narrow, barely wide enough for a single person to pass. Ragnar went first, his spectral form easily slipping through the opening. The others followed, their senses heightened, their weapons at the ready.

The air inside was thick with the scent of damp earth and decay, the silence broken only by the drip of water from the crumbling ceiling. The structure was circular, its walls lined with shelves upon which lay broken pottery shards and rusted metal objects. In the center of the room, a low stone altar stood, its surface covered in a layer of dust and debris.

It was Leif, his keen eye for detail, who spotted the first clue. Etched into the altar's surface was a series of runes, ancient symbols that shimmered faintly in the dim light. Harald, with his knowledge of ancient Norse lore, recognized them immediately. "The runes of Morwen," he whispered, his voice filled with a chilling recognition. "Her mark. She was here."

As they deciphered the runes, a horrifying story unfolded, revealing a deeper understanding of the massacre and Morwen's motivations. The writings detailed Morwen's obsession with resurrecting a powerful demon warlord, a being of unimaginable power capable of reshaping the world according to her twisted desires. The island, they discovered, was not simply the site of a massacre but a crucial part of her ritual, a place where the veil between worlds was thin, where the dark magic that powered her plans held sway.

The Vikings, it turned out, had stumbled upon Morwen's plans, inadvertently disrupting her rituals. Their deaths, while brutal, were a necessary sacrifice in her eyes, a cleansing that would pave the way for the demon warlord's resurrection. The locket, it was revealed, was not merely a prison for their souls but also a key, a conduit through which Morwen would channel her dark magic.

Beyond the main chamber, they discovered a hidden passage, a narrow, twisting corridor that led to a series of smaller chambers. Here, they found more ancient writings, fragments of maps, and strange artifacts – remnants of Morwen's rituals and experiments. One chamber held a collection of bones, meticulously arranged in a disturbing pattern. Another contained a series of alchemical concoctions, their viscous liquids bubbling gently in their aged containers.

The discovery of these artifacts provided further clues about Morwen's power and her methods. They revealed the extent of her depravity, her unwavering pursuit of power at any cost. The Vikings' sacrifice had not been random; it had been a calculated act, a necessary step in her demonic plan. Elias felt a wave of nausea, the sheer horror of her actions washing over him.

The most significant discovery was a hidden alcove behind the altar. Inside, they found a small, leather-bound book. Its pages, brittle with age, contained a series of spells and incantations, the very essence of Morwen's dark magic. The book detailed the process of the ritual, the precise steps needed to unleash the demon warlord upon the world, and a counter-spell, a desperate attempt by the Vikings to thwart her plans. The counter-spell was incomplete, half-finished, but it offered a glimmer of hope, a possible way to prevent the coming catastrophe.

As they studied the book's contents, the Vikings' memories flooded Elias's mind, revealing their final moments, their valiant fight against insurmountable odds. He saw their fear, their despair, but also their unwavering courage, their determination to protect their land, their people. He felt their rage, their sorrow, their undying loyalty to one another, a bond that transcended even death itself.

The island of shadows had revealed its secrets, unveiling a deeper understanding of the past, the events that had led to this perilous moment. But the knowledge they gained came at a price. The weight of their collective destiny pressed down upon them, the enormity of the task ahead almost unbearable. The blood moon hung high in the sky, its crimson glow casting long, menacing shadows, a stark reminder of the approaching deadline. The final confrontation was imminent, and the fate of the kingdom, and perhaps the world, rested on their shoulders. They emerged from the ruins, the mist swirling around them, carrying with them a burden of knowledge, a determination fueled by the memories of fallen warriors and a shared sense of impending doom. The race against time had begun.

The mist thinned as they emerged from the ruins, revealing a stark, desolate landscape stretching before them. The blood moon cast an eerie glow upon the twisted trees and the barren earth, painting the scene in shades of crimson and shadow. It was in this desolate expanse that they encountered Morwen's lieutenant – a hulking figure clad in black armour, his face obscured by a horned helmet that seemed to writhe with a dark energy.

He stood sentinel before a chasm that yawned before them, a gaping maw in the earth that seemed to breathe with an unnatural darkness. The air crackled with arcane energy, a palpable sense of dread emanating from the lieutenant and the chasm alike. This was no ordinary warrior; this was a creature of shadow and dark magic, a testament to Morwen's unholy power.

The lieutenant moved with unnatural speed, a blur of black armour and lethal grace. He raised a hand, and from the depths of the chasm, skeletal creatures clawed their way upwards, their bony fingers scraping against the earth with a grating sound that sent shivers down their spines. These were not mere undead; they moved with a disturbing intelligence, their eyes burning with malevolent green fire. They were Morwen's thralls, her dark creations, brought to life by her unholy magic.

Ragnar, ever the seasoned warrior, roared a challenge, his spectral sword flashing in the moonlight. He charged, his spectral form a whirlwind of furious attacks, his blade singing a death song as it cleaved through the skeletal horde. Bjorn followed close behind, his brute strength amplified by the locket, his every blow shattering bones and sending skeletal fragments flying. Harald and Leif, despite their ethereal forms, fought with a ferocity that belied their spectral existence, their skills honed over centuries of warfare.

Elias, however, found himself struggling. The lieutenant's power was far greater than anything he had encountered before. The skeletal creatures were relentless, their numbers seemingly endless, and the lieutenant himself moved with an unnerving preternatural speed, his attacks precise and deadly. Elias, despite his newfound strength and the Vikings' memories guiding him, felt overwhelmed. He was strong, yes, but he was still a novice, a mere vessel for ancient warriors, pitted against a seasoned servant of dark magic.

The lieutenant's weapon was not a sword or an axe, but a staff of twisted black wood, pulsing with a dark, malevolent energy. With each swing, the staff unleashed blasts of dark magic that sent shockwaves rippling through the air, pushing Elias back, burning his skin, and draining his strength. He stumbled, his legs giving way beneath him, the weight of the battle threatening to crush him.

It was in his moment of weakness that he felt the Vikings surge forward, their memories, their skills, and their courage flooding his being. They were not merely memories now, but extensions of himself, a part of his very being. Ragnar's strategic mind guided his movements, Bjorn's raw strength bolstered his blows, and Harald and Leif's tactical prowess sharpened his reactions.

Suddenly, Elias felt a surge of power, a surge that transcended his human limits. His movements became fluid, his reactions instantaneous, his senses heightened. He moved with a grace and power that surprised even himself, his every move a reflection of the Vikings' combined skill and experience. He parried a blow from the lieutenant's staff, the impact sending tremors up his arms. The force of the blow was immense, but he held. He was no longer simply Elias, but Elias and the five Vikings, a force far greater than the sum of its parts.

The battle raged on, a chaotic dance of steel and dark magic, a clash of ancient power and newfound strength. The skeletal horde continued their assault, a relentless tide of bone and shadow, but Elias, empowered by the Vikings' spirits, fought with a renewed determination. He dodged, weaved, and counterattacked, his sword singing a deadly symphony, each strike precise and deadly.

The lieutenant, however, remained a formidable opponent. He seemed to anticipate Elias's every move, his defenses impenetrable. His dark magic was relentless, draining Elias's strength with each attack, leaving him feeling drained and vulnerable. The chasm itself seemed to amplify his power, drawing strength from its depths.

Elias realized he could not defeat the lieutenant through brute force. He needed a strategy, a plan that would exploit the lieutenant's weaknesses, a tactic that would leverage the unique blend of powers now residing within him. He observed the lieutenant carefully, noting his movements, his patterns, his limitations. He saw the reliance on his dark magic, the drain on his own power with each extravagant gesture.

In a moment of clarity, inspired by Harald's tactical genius, Elias launched a deceptive maneuver, feigning weakness, luring the lieutenant in with a carefully crafted feint. He drew the lieutenant close, allowing the lieutenant to unleash a concentrated blast of dark magic, but instead of dodging, Elias channeled the energy, letting it surge through him, absorbing it into his own power. It was a dangerous gamble, akin to walking a tightrope above a chasm, but Elias felt the power of the five Vikings surging in him, guiding his every instinct.

The energy coursed through him, a potent wave of dark magic now intertwined with his own, amplifying his strength and resilience. It felt like the power of the blood moon itself flowing through his veins, a celestial energy he never thought he could control. He roared, a sound echoing the combined strength of five fallen warriors, and unleashed a counter-attack.

The blow, empowered by the absorbed dark magic, struck the lieutenant with ferocious power. The impact sent the lieutenant reeling back, his black armour cracking, his dark staff shattering into splinters. He stumbled back, his form flickering and unstable, his grip on his dark magic weakening. The skeletal horde, sensing their master's weakening power, began to disintegrate, their bony forms collapsing into dust.

The lieutenant, defeated, collapsed to his knees, his supernatural powers failing. He was not dead, but his influence was broken. The chasm behind him seemed to shrink, its dark energy receding, its power diminished.

The battle was won, but the victory was hard-earned. Elias, drained but victorious, stood over the fallen lieutenant, his breathing ragged, his body aching. He knew this was merely a step in their greater journey. The island was a maze of challenges, and Morwen's power still stretched far. But for now, they had gained a crucial advantage. The way to the blood moon ritual was one step closer, but the path remained treacherous. The blood moon was still high in the sky, its crimson glow a constant reminder of the deadline fast approaching.

The greatest battle was yet to come.

The lieutenant's defeat left a heavy silence hanging in the air, broken only by the mournful sigh of the wind whistling through the skeletal remains of Morwen's army. The chasm behind the fallen figure had shrunk considerably, its ominous aura diminished to a faint whisper of darkness. Elias, leaning heavily on his sword, felt the lingering exhaustion of the battle, the combined drain of his own strength and the energy he had absorbed from the lieutenant. The five Vikings within him were silent, their usual boisterous energy replaced with a cautious stillness. They knew the victory was fleeting, a mere respite in a much larger conflict.

Ragnar, his voice a low rumble in Elias's mind, broke the silence. "We must press on. The lieutenant guarded more than just this path; he guarded the key to Morwen's weakness."

Bjorn, ever practical, added, "And that key, I suspect, lies within the heart of this accursed island."

Following the lieutenant's defeated form, they began to search the surrounding area for any sign of what Ragnar alluded to, a way past the immediate danger. The terrain was treacherous, the ground uneven and littered with sharp rocks. The trees, twisted and gnarled, seemed to reach out with skeletal branches, their shadows dancing in the eerie glow of the blood moon. The air itself felt heavy, charged with an unsettling stillness that was far more threatening than the battle they had just fought.

Their search led them to a hidden cavern, concealed behind a waterfall that cascaded down the cliff face. The roar of the water masked the entrance, cleverly disguised by nature's own hand. The Vikings, their memories of ancient battles and hidden passages surfacing, guided Elias towards the waterfall's base. The water was icy cold, a shock that sent shivers through Elias, even with the strength of the Vikings coursing through his veins.

The cavern opened into a vast, echoing chamber. Torches, magically sustained, illuminated the space, revealing intricate carvings on the cavern walls, depictions of ancient rituals and battles. The air within was thick with the scent of damp earth and something else... something ancient, something powerful. It was a palpable sense of history, the weight of ages pressing down on them.

The cavern floor was a labyrinth of pathways, intricate and confusing. Each step was a careful calculation, for the floor was riddled with traps, cleverly concealed beneath layers of dust and debris. Pressure plates triggered showers of razor-sharp stones, while tripwires unleashed nets of woven thorns, designed to entangle and ensnare. Leif, whose memories were particularly adept at deciphering ancient puzzles and traps, guided Elias, his spectral form flitting ahead, carefully disarming each deadly snare.

Days bled into nights as they navigated this subterranean maze, each passage leading to a new challenge. They encountered intricate puzzles, their solutions hidden within the cryptic carvings on the walls. Harald, with his keen intellect and centuries of experience, deciphered the riddles, his knowledge guiding Elias towards the correct path. These were not mere riddles; they were tests of wit, designed to challenge the intellect as much as the physical strength.

Alistair stepped forward, brushing soot from the stone's surface with a practiced hand. "This sigil," he said, pointing to an angular rune, "was only used in pre-collapse texts. It's not just a warning — it's a map." He looked up, eyes sharp. "Morwen didn't just awaken the curse. She's following something older."

Finally, after what seemed like an eternity, they reached the heart of the cavern. Before them stood a massive stone altar, etched with runes that pulsed with a faint, ethereal glow. Upon the altar rested a small, ornate wooden box, secured by intricate locks and bound with chains of silver, each link engraved with symbols of protection. This was the artifact. This was the key.

The box exuded a powerful energy, a palpable hum that vibrated through the very stones of the cavern. Elias felt a surge of energy within him, the five Vikings stirring with excitement and anticipation. This was no ordinary artifact; it was imbued with ancient power, a relic of a bygone era, its power capable of shifting the tide of their current battle.

The locks were ancient and complex, protected by powerful enchantments. The silver chains were enchanted to resist any force that tried to break them, seemingly impenetrable. The combined strength of the five Vikings, even channeled through Elias, barely made a dent. It was clear that brute force alone would not suffice.

It was then that Elias recalled a passage from the cavern walls, a cryptic inscription that spoke of a hidden melody, a song of power capable of unlocking the box. He remembered the eerie tune the lieutenant's staff seemed to emit. The eerie tune was a key to unlocking the artifact, a connection he had missed until this very moment.

He closed his eyes, focusing on the inscription, the cryptic melody resonating within his mind. He drew upon the memories of the Vikings, drawing on their ancient musical traditions, their knowledge of ancient runes and their understanding of the mystical arts. He summoned the melody, singing a song of ancient power, his voice filled with the haunting echo of the fallen warriors. It was a mournful, ethereal tune, a lament for those lost to the darkness, yet imbued with a power that vibrated through the cavern.

As Elias sang, the runes on the altar began to glow brighter, the box on the altar responding to the ancient song. The locks clicked open one by one, the silver chains dissolving into shimmering dust. The ancient magic, awakened by the correct melody, released the artifact's protective enchantments. The box, now open, revealed a single, smooth black stone, pulsing with an inner light, a deep energy that felt both ancient and incredibly powerful. The artifact was far more simple than they had anticipated, its power disguised by a deceptive exterior.

As Elias reached for the stone, a wave of raw, untamed power washed over him, almost knocking him off his feet. The stone felt warm to the touch, its surface smooth and cool against his skin. As he grasped it, visions flooded his mind – visions of the island's past, of Morwen's rise to power, of the ancient battles fought upon this very land. The stone seemed to resonate with his own energies and the energies of the five Vikings, amplifying their strength and capabilities in a completely unexpected way.

He felt a connection, a deep understanding of the stone's purpose, its potential. This was not simply a weapon; it was a key, a tool capable of weakening Morwen's power. The stone pulsing with raw arcane energy was far more powerful than he imagined. It was a weapon forged in ancient times, capable of turning the tide of the upcoming battle.

With the artifact secured, Elias and the Vikings prepared for the final confrontation. They emerged from the cavern, their hearts filled with a cautious optimism. The blood moon hung high in the sky, its crimson glow casting a menacing shadow over the island.

Their journey was far from over, but with the hidden artifact in hand, they were now one step closer to confronting Morwen and ending her reign of terror. The final battle was fast approaching. The fate of the kingdom rested on their shoulders. The weight of the world felt heavy upon them, but they were ready. They were prepared. They would face Morwen. They would face the demons. They would prevail.

The black stone pulsed in Elias's hand, a warm thrumming against his palm that mirrored the unsettling rhythm of his own heart. The visions it had unleashed—flashes of brutal battles, of a woman's chilling laughter echoing across a blood-soaked battlefield, of the Vikings' own agonizing deaths—were fading, leaving behind a lingering residue of fear and despair. He clutched the stone tighter, seeking solace in its tangible presence, yet finding only a growing unease.

The journey out of the cavern felt longer than the descent. The Vikings, usually boisterous in their spectral forms, were subdued, their ghostly voices a hushed murmur in Elias's mind. They were silent witnesses to the visions, their shared past resurrected in a way none of them could have anticipated. Their silence was heavier than any battle cry.

Ragnar, the leader, spoke first, his voice a low tremor that vibrated through Elias's very bones. "Morwen's power... it's ancient, Elias. Older than any of us can comprehend. This stone... it is a key, yes, but also a burden."

Bjorn, ever practical, echoed Ragnar's apprehension. "The visions... they show not only Morwen's strength, but the depth of her cruelty. She is a master of manipulation, twisting events and weaving illusions to her advantage. We must be prepared for anything."

Leif, usually the jovial one, was consumed by a haunted silence, his spectral form flickering like a dying ember. The memories of his death, vividly relived through the stone, had apparently shaken him to his core. He was barely participating in the conversation.

Harald, ever the intellectual, spoke in a measured tone. "The runes on the altar... they spoke of a prophecy, a foretold battle between light and darkness. Morwen sought to tip the balance, to unleash a power that would consume the world. We are caught in the midst of this ancient struggle."

The weight of their words settled upon Elias like a physical burden. He had initially embraced the power of the Vikings, their strength a welcome addition to his own meager abilities. Now, however, he felt the chilling weight of their history, their tragedies, their ultimate defeat. He was no longer just carrying their souls; he was carrying their past, their pain, their unresolved conflicts.

The island itself seemed to mirror his internal turmoil. The wind howled through the skeletal remains of Morwen's army, the whispers of the dead intertwining with the Vikings' own ghostly voices. The blood moon, a malevolent eye in the night sky, cast long, menacing shadows that seemed to writhe and shift.

As they emerged from the cavern, the full extent of the island's desolation became apparent. The once vibrant landscape was now a charred wasteland, scarred by ancient battles and choked by the insidious growth of Morwen's dark magic. The very air crackled with an unnatural energy, a tangible sense of dread that seeped into Elias's bones.

Elias felt the growing unease amongst his companions. The weight of their past, the visions of their deaths, and the sheer scale of Morwen's evil were threatening to consume them all. Even the usually stoic Ragnar looked shaken. Bjorn seemed to be considering the possible tactical implications of their latest revelation, his usual calmness strained to its limits. Leif and Harald both stared at the island in horrified awe, the magnitude of their enemy's power sinking in. The weight of the battle ahead rested heavily upon each of their shoulders.

That night, under the crimson glare of the blood moon, Elias found himself alone, the black stone clutched tightly in his hand. The visions returned, more vivid and more disturbing than before. He saw Morwen, her face a mask of cruel ambition, orchestrating the massacre of the Vikings, her laughter echoing across the blood-soaked battlefield. He felt the sting of their weapons, the searing pain of their deaths, and the chilling emptiness of their final moments.

He saw not only their deaths but also the betrayal, the manipulation that led to their downfall. He saw glimpses of internal conflicts, rivalries amongst the Vikings that had been cleverly exploited by Morwen to ensure her victory. The visions also revealed glimpses of the demon warlord Morwen aimed to resurrect, a being of unimaginable power, whose release would mean the complete destruction of the realm. The weight of all this information was almost unbearable.

The physical and emotional toll was immense. Elias felt the strain on his body, his muscles aching, his energy depleted. But it was the emotional burden that proved the most difficult to bear. He battled with nightmares, visions of Morwen's triumphant grin repeating over and over again. It was a torture far worse than any physical wound.

He questioned his own ability to carry this burden, to shoulder the weight of their past and the responsibility of their future. Was he truly worthy of their strength, their trust, their sacrifices? Could he truly be the one to defeat Morwen, to stop her from unleashing the demon warlord? Could he handle the weight of the world placed on his shoulders? Doubt, insidious and pervasive, began to creep into his mind.

He looked at the stone, the source of his power, yet also the source of his torment. Was it a gift or a curse? He contemplated throwing it away, hoping to escape the burden, to return to his old life, his own insignificant existence before the Vikings became his unwilling companions. The very thought, however, felt treacherous, like abandoning his friends to a fate he could have prevented.

As the first rays of dawn painted the sky with streaks of pale light, Elias knew he couldn't run. He could not abandon the Vikings who had placed their faith, their lives, in him. He had to accept the weight of their past, their pain, their hopes and fight for their redemption. The responsibility felt as heavy as mountains. It was a burden he would have to bear, not out of obligation, but out of a newfound respect and understanding of the sacrifice they had made. The journey ahead would be arduous, but he would persevere. He would face whatever came his way. He would face Morwen. The weight of the past had broken him, but it had also forged something new within him: a strength born not just of the Vikings' power, but of his own resolve, his own fierce determination.

The black stone burned warmly in his hand, and Elias knew that he would use it well. The struggle to overcome Morwen was just beginning. The fate of the kingdom and the world lay in his hands. He would not falter. He would not fail. He would fight. He would prevail.

The sun, a pale disc barely visible through the persistent gloom that clung to the island, offered little warmth. Elias, his body still aching from the emotional and physical toll of the previous night's visions, knew he couldn't rely on the Vikings' strength alone. He needed allies, and the whispers of the island's hidden inhabitants offered a sliver of hope. The monks of the Silent Order, secluded in their mountain monastery, were legendary for their arcane knowledge; their rumored mastery of ancient magic could prove invaluable. But reaching them would be no easy feat. Their monastery was said to be guarded by treacherous paths and even more treacherous guardians—creatures born of the island's dark magic, twisted and warped by Morwen's influence.

The first leg of his journey took him through a blighted forest, where skeletal trees clawed at the sky like the grasping hands of the dead. The air hung heavy with the stench of decay and the unsettling silence that only death could bring. Elias felt the Vikings' spectral forms tense beside him, their ghostly senses alert to the unseen dangers lurking in the shadows. Ragnar, his voice a low growl in Elias's mind, warned of illusions and traps, the remnants of Morwen's ancient magic still clinging to the land, twisting perceptions and blurring reality.

They encountered twisted, thorny vines that lashed out with surprising strength, their barbs laced with a venom that left burning trails on Elias's skin. Bjorn, despite his spectral form, expertly guided Elias through the thicket, his ghostly hands parting the thorny branches with a skill honed over centuries of battle. They navigated treacherous ravines where the earth itself seemed to crumble beneath their feet, their ghostly footsteps echoing eerily in the void. Harald, ever the strategist, identified weak points in the landscape, charting a course that minimized their exposure to the ever-present dangers.

As they pressed onward, the forest grew denser, the shadows deeper. Elias felt a prickling sensation on his skin, a sense of being watched, of unseen eyes following their every move. Leif, normally the most jovial of the Vikings, felt the tension acutely, his ghostly form flickering nervously. He warned Elias of the forest's guardians— creatures shaped from the island's very essence, twisted and warped into grotesque parodies of life. These were not mere beasts, but sentient beings born from Morwen's dark magic, driven by an instinctive hatred of all that opposed her.

They encountered their first guardian at dusk. It was a creature of nightmare, a grotesque amalgamation of twisted branches and razor-sharp thorns, its form shifting and changing with unsettling fluidity. Its eyes, glowing embers in the deepening twilight, fixed on Elias with malevolent intent. The creature lunged, its thorny limbs whipping through the air with surprising speed. The Vikings, their spectral forms ablaze with ethereal energy, fought with a ferocity that belied their ghostly state. Bjorn's ghostly axe cleaved through the creature's thorny limbs, while Ragnar's spectral sword unleashed a barrage of ghostly blows. Harald's ghostly spells weaved a protective barrier around Elias, shielding him from the creature's venomous attacks. Even Leif, despite his initial fear, found his courage and fought with surprising strength. The battle was fierce, a whirlwind of ghostly blows and desperate parries. Elias, fueled by the Vikings' power and his own growing determination, found a strength he never knew he possessed. He fought alongside his ghostly companions, their combined might pushing back against the creature's relentless assault. Finally, with a mighty blow from Ragnar, the creature succumbed, its form dissolving into a cloud of black smoke that vanished into the shadows.

Exhausted but unbroken, they pressed on, their journey leading them to the treacherous mountain path that led to the Silent Order's monastery. The ascent was arduous, the path winding precariously along cliffsides that plunged into bottomless chasms. The wind howled fiercely, threatening to sweep them into the abyss. Elias, his muscles burning, his breath ragged, clung to the rock face, the Vikings' spectral forms supporting him, their ghostly hands helping him to maintain his grip.

Finally, after what seemed like an eternity, they reached the monastery, a solitary structure clinging to the mountainside like a brooding bird of prey. The air around the monastery was different – still, serene, yet charged with an almost palpable energy. The monastery itself was a marvel of ancient architecture, its stone walls weathered by time, but radiating a sense of unwavering strength.

Approaching the monastery gates, Elias felt a sense of apprehension. The monks of the Silent Order were renowned for their reclusive nature, their deep-seated aversion to outsiders. Gaining their trust would require more than just strength; it would require diplomacy, patience, and perhaps even a touch of deception. The fate of the kingdom, perhaps even the world, rested on his ability to forge this unlikely alliance.

Their arrival at the monastery was met with silent observation. Shadowy figures moved within the walls, their eyes like dark pools watching their approach. After a tense moment, the massive wooden gates creaked open, revealing a courtyard filled with an almost palpable aura of tranquility. A figure emerged, cloaked in robes of deep brown, his face hidden in shadow. This was Brother Thomas, the Order's spokesperson, a man whose reputation for wisdom was matched only by his reputation for impassivity.

Elias presented his case, explaining the looming threat of Morwen and her plans for the demon warlord. He spoke of the visions he had received, the battles he had witnessed, the burdens he now carried. Brother Thomas listened with stoic patience, his expression giving nothing away. He raised no objections to the unusual nature of Elias' claims, nor did he display any sign of disbelief. It was clear he was not easily fooled or swayed by rhetoric. His silence was unnerving, yet there was a subtle sense of understanding behind it.

After what felt like an eternity, Brother Thomas spoke, his voice low and measured, "The prophecy speaks of a champion, one who would unite the disparate factions against the encroaching darkness. You have borne witness to the past. Now you must shape the future." His words were a tacit acceptance, an acknowledgment of Elias's destiny, but also a solemn warning of the path ahead.

With the monks' reluctant support secured, Elias turned his attention to the other element of his alliance: the Blood Ravens, a mercenary company known for their brutal efficiency and unwavering loyalty, led by the enigmatic Captain Valeria. Finding them proved to be a different kind of challenge, requiring a journey through treacherous swamps and across the mountains. Their camp was a sight of controlled chaos, a testament to their ruthless effectiveness.

Their leader, Captain Valeria, a woman whose eyes held the icy glint of a winter storm, met Elias with a skeptical gaze. Elias had to convince Valeria that his cause was worthy of their assistance; he had to appeal not just to her sense of loyalty, but also to her innate pragmatism. He spoke of the riches Morwen possessed, the treasures that could secure their future. The Blood Ravens, after all, were mercenaries, not crusaders. Valeria, assessing the situation with cold eyes, saw the potential for gain and a chance for a glorious victory that would add to their reputation. With a curt nod, she agreed to join his cause. The alliance, forged in necessity and ambition, was complete. Elias, though his path still perilous, was no longer alone. He had allies now, unlikely allies, but allies nonetheless, and his chance of facing Morwen, and winning, felt a little stronger. The weight of the world, though still heavy, felt slightly less crushing. The battle for the kingdom's survival, the world's survival, was truly underway.

Brother Thomas, his face still obscured by shadow, gestured towards a worn, leather-bound book resting on a simple wooden table. The air around the book hummed with a faint, almost imperceptible energy, a silent testament to its age and power. He opened it carefully, revealing pages filled with faded script, intricate diagrams, and illustrations of creatures both terrifying and awe-inspiring. The parchment, brittle with age, crackled softly as he turned the pages, each rustle echoing in the hushed silence of the chamber.

"This," Brother Thomas said, his voice a low murmur, "is the Chronicon Daemonium, a chronicle of the demon warlord, Malkor, whose soul Morwen seeks to resurrect."

The Chronicon Daemonium detailed Malkor's rise and fall, a tale woven with threads of dark magic and unspeakable cruelty. He was not merely a demon, but a being of immense power, a creature of shadow and fire, whose very presence warped the fabric of reality. The monks had painstakingly preserved the chronicle for centuries, safeguarding its secrets from those who would misuse its knowledge. The book revealed that Malkor's power was intrinsically linked to a ritualistic object – a obsidian dagger forged in the heart of a dying star, imbued with the essence of a fallen god. Only by possessing and destroying the dagger could Malkor's resurrection be prevented.

"Morwen's ultimate goal is to use this dagger to anchor Malkor's soul to the mortal realm," Brother Thomas explained, his eyes flickering with a faint inner light. "The blood moon ritual she plans is not merely a summoning, but a binding, a fusion of demonic power with the physical world. Should she succeed, Malkor's influence would corrupt the very essence of existence, transforming this land into a blighted wasteland mirroring the hellscape from which he came."

The monks' wisdom extended beyond the simple narrative of Malkor's existence. They revealed details of his weaknesses, gleaned from centuries of study and deciphered from cryptic prophecies. Malkor, despite his immense power, possessed vulnerabilities. He was susceptible to certain types of ancient magic, spells woven with the threads of forgotten gods and lost languages. The monks possessed scrolls and grimoires detailing these potent incantations, but mastering them would require immense skill, dedication, and a deep understanding of arcane lore.

Elias, his mind reeling from the sheer weight of the information, felt a sense of daunting responsibility. The task ahead was not merely to confront Morwen; it was to unravel centuries of dark history, to decipher ancient prophecies, and to master powerful magic in a race against time. He felt the spectral forms of the Vikings stir beside him, their ghostly senses picking up the vibrations of the ancient knowledge, their ethereal minds absorbing the information with an uncanny speed.

"The obsidian dagger," Brother Thomas continued, his voice regaining its measured calm, "is hidden within Morwen's stronghold, guarded by creatures born from her darkest magic and loyal servants twisted into horrifying parodies of their former selves." He paused, his gaze piercing Elias's soul. "To retrieve the dagger will require stealth, cunning, and a strength far exceeding that of a mortal man. But you are not merely a mortal man, Elias. You carry within you the souls of warriors, each with unique talents and skills."

The monks then delved into the history of the obsidian dagger itself, revealing its origins and the terrible power it contained. It was said to have been crafted by a fallen god, a being of immense power who had rebelled against the celestial order. This god, consumed by his own ambition and pride, had been banished to the void between worlds, his essence infused into the dagger. The dagger, therefore, possessed not only the power to bind Malkor, but also the potential to unleash unimaginable devastation. The monks emphasized the delicate nature of wielding such power. It was a double-edged sword, capable of both saving the realm and destroying it.

The monks revealed that the dagger was not merely an instrument of power, but also a key. It was the key to a hidden chamber beneath Morwen's fortress, a chamber containing another powerful artifact: a mystical amulet said to possess the power to dispel demonic influence. The amulet, known as the Sunstone, was a beacon of light and purity, a counterpoint to Malkor's dark energy.

The monks provided Elias with a detailed map, painstakingly drawn and annotated with cryptic symbols. The map depicted the treacherous route leading to Morwen's stronghold, highlighting hidden passages, perilous obstacles, and the locations of Morwen's guardians. They provided Elias with scrolls containing protective spells, wards against dark magic, and instructions on how to navigate the treacherous landscape. The monks stressed the necessity of caution; Morwen's fortress was a labyrinth of deception, where illusions masked reality, and the line between truth and falsehood blurred.

Furthermore, the monks shared a disturbing piece of information. Morwen was not working alone. She had formed an alliance with a shadowy cabal of necromancers and sorcerers, each wielding their own unique brand of dark magic. These individuals were powerful in their own right, capable of inflicting significant harm. The monks advised Elias to approach the task with utmost caution and vigilance, to be prepared for any eventuality. They stressed the importance of strategy and teamwork, urging him to rely on the strengths of his allies, both living and spectral.

The monks, their faces illuminated by the faint glow of candlelight, also imparted knowledge of ancient rituals that could weaken Malkor's hold on the world. They spoke of sacred sites, forgotten groves, and ancient burial grounds, where specific incantations and offerings could disrupt his power, rendering him more vulnerable when he was eventually confronted. The monks stressed the importance of timing, the precise alignment of stars and the phases of the moon playing crucial roles in the success of these rituals.

The meeting with the monks was not just a source of information, it was a transformative experience. Elias, already changed by the

Vikings' presence, now felt a profound connection to the ancient history and the weight of the prophecies. He left the monastery a changed man, carrying the weight of the world, the knowledge of the past, and the hope of a future he now had the power to shape.

He knew the path ahead was fraught with danger, but the knowledge gained from the monks gave him a new resolve, a new understanding of the fight that lay before him. He was not merely fighting Morwen; he was fighting against the darkness itself, a fight that spanned centuries and threatened the very fabric of existence.

The weight of his responsibility was immense, but with the wisdom of the monks, and the strength of his unlikely allies, Elias knew he had a fighting chance.

The air hung thick with the scent of sweat, blood, and woodsmoke. The training grounds of the Silver Eagles mercenaries were a brutal testament to the unforgiving nature of their profession. Elias, his Viking companions swirling around him like restless spirits, found himself thrust into a world of relentless physical and mental exertion. He was no longer the quiet, unassuming outcast; he was a whirlwind of motion, a blur of steel and fury, guided by the centuries of combat experience ingrained within him by the warriors' souls.

Ragnar, the eldest of the Vikings, a towering figure even in spectral form, oversaw their training with a steely gaze. His voice, a low rumble that resonated deep within Elias's bones, provided constant instruction and critique. "Precision, Elias," he'd growl, his spectral hand a phantom correcting Elias's stance. "The blade is an extension of your will. Let your fury be your guide, but control it, lest it consumes you."

Bjorn, the fierce warrior, focused on honing Elias's raw strength. He pushed Elias to his absolute limit, sparring sessions that felt less like practice and more like actual battles to the death. Bjorn's spectral blows were surprisingly tangible, leaving Elias aching and bruised, yet invigorated by the sheer power they unleashed. "Strength without control is meaningless," Bjorn would bellow, his spectral form a blur of motion as he parried and thrust. "You must be as swift as a viper, as strong as a bear, and as resilient as the granite mountains."

Leif, the cunning strategist, focused on tactical combat and coordinated movements. He schooled Elias and his companions in the art of deception, ambush, and coordinated assaults, utilizing the terrain to their advantage. "Victory is not won through brute force alone," Leif would whisper, his spectral eyes gleaming with tactical brilliance as he plotted manoeuvres on the dusty ground. "It's won through strategy, patience, and the exploitation of weakness."

Hroar, the master archer, patiently instructed Elias in the art of ranged combat. Initially, Elias struggled, the bow feeling unwieldy in his hands. But Hroar's spectral guidance, almost a physical presence in his mind's eye, gradually improved his aim, his shots becoming increasingly accurate and deadly. "Your enemies will not always be within arms reach," Hroar advised. "A well-placed arrow can be as effective as any sword."

Finally, there was Ivar, the silent observer, the master of stealth and infiltration. He taught Elias the nuances of shadow and silence, how to move without being detected, how to blend with the darkness, becoming one with the night itself. Ivar's spectral presence was a constant reminder that the most effective battles were often fought before they even began, in the realm of covert operations and strategic subterfuge. Ivar's lessons were less about physical prowess and more about patience, observation, and unwavering focus.

Their training wasn't limited to individual combat. The mercenaries subjected Elias and his companions to grueling exercises focused on group coordination and teamwork. They practiced intricate formations, coordinated attacks, and defensive maneuvers designed to maximize their collective strength. They learned to anticipate each other's movements, to rely on each other implicitly, to fight as one cohesive unit. Mock battles, simulations of actual combat scenarios, pitted them against skilled mercenaries, testing their ability to adapt, to strategize, and to overcome adversity. The Silver Eagles spared no expense, pushing them to their absolute limits.

They faced down waves of enemies, navigated complex terrains, and dealt with surprise attacks. The training was brutal, designed to mold them into a finely tuned fighting machine.

The mercenaries' training methods went beyond pure combat skills.

They incorporated rigorous physical conditioning, demanding stamina and endurance exercises that stretched Elias's body to its breaking point. Long marches, cross-country runs, and intense weight-training sessions tested Elias's resolve, forging a resilience that matched his newfound physical prowess. Their mental conditioning was just as relentless. They endured sleep deprivation, sensory overload, and psychological stress tests, designed to break their will and expose their vulnerabilities. But the Vikings, in their spectral forms, were constant sources of strength, their collective experience providing an internal resilience that helped Elias withstand the unrelenting pressure. They pushed each other, spurred each other on, and never faltered in their commitment.

The nights were filled with strategy sessions, poring over maps, studying enemy tactics, and refining their own battle plans. The mercenaries shared their vast experience, detailing battles fought and won, lessons learned and mistakes avoided. Elias absorbed their knowledge like a sponge, his mind racing to assimilate the sheer volume of information. He found himself thinking in strategies, anticipating enemy maneuvers, and adapting his tactics with a speed that surprised even himself. The spectral presence of the Vikings allowed him to receive and process information at a vastly accelerated rate, a unique advantage that amplified their training.

As the weeks turned into months, Elias and his companions underwent a complete transformation. They were no longer mere outcasts; they were elite warriors, refined and honed by the Silver Eagles. Their individual skills blended seamlessly into a powerful collective, their synergy a terrifying testament to their training. They mastered various weapon systems: swords, axes, spears, bows, and crossbows, learning to adapt their fighting style to any situation. They learned to use the terrain to their advantage, using cover and concealment effectively, and to exploit weak points in enemy formations. They learned to cooperate, to trust each other, and to rely on their team's collective strength to accomplish tasks.

The final test arrived without warning – a brutal, all-out assault against a fortified mercenary camp manned by the Silver Eagles' own elite forces. The battle was chaotic, a maelstrom of steel and fury, where Elias found himself engaging in relentless combat, facing overwhelming odds, his every move guided by the ghostly warriors within him. He fought with a savagery that surprised even himself, his movements fluid and precise, his attacks relentless and deadly. The

Viking's spirits fought alongside him, their spectral forms blending seamlessly with his own, their collective power making him an almost invincible force. He felt their strength coursing through his veins, their experience guiding his every action. The battle was a crucible, a final test that forged their bond and prepared them for the confrontation with Morwen. They fought as one, a single unit, mirroring the seamless teamwork they had developed during months of brutal training.

They emerged victorious, exhausted but triumphant, their bodies battered but their spirits unbroken. The Silver Eagles, impressed by their performance, congratulated them, acknowledging their transformation. They were ready. The final battle loomed, and they were prepared to confront Morwen and her demonic forces with courage, skill, and the unwavering bond forged in the fires of intense mercenary training. They had evolved, not just physically and tactically but also as a team, a cohesive unit bound together by their shared trials and triumphs. The ancient warriors' spirits within Elias had found a perfect vessel, and he, in turn, had found his purpose: the fight against a darkness that threatened to consume the world. The weight of responsibility rested on his shoulders, but he carried it with the strength of five warriors, guided by the wisdom of seasoned mercenaries, and the unwavering support of his companions.

The air in the ancient monastery, thick with the scent of incense and old parchment, hung heavy with the weight of centuries. Brother Thomas, his face etched with the wisdom of countless years spent deciphering forgotten texts, traced a finger across a faded map. Elias, Ragnar, Bjorn, Leif, Hroar, and Ivar stood around him, the spectral forms of the Viking warriors flickering faintly in the candlelight. The mercenary training had left them physically and mentally exhausted, yet the urgency of the situation kept them alert, their senses sharpened. They needed answers, and Brother Thomas, with his encyclopedic knowledge of arcane lore, was their only hope.

"Morwen's ritual," Brother Thomas began, his voice a low, resonant hum, "is far more than a simple summoning. It's a key, a gateway to unleashing a power that has been dormant for millennia." He gestured to the map, a complex network of lines and symbols that seemed to pulse with a faint, inner light. "This," he explained, "is the location – Cairn of Whispers, a desolate isle shrouded in perpetual mist, a place of ancient power and forgotten magic."

The map showed a remote island, marked with a peculiar symbol –a crescent moon bisected by a jagged line. The symbol seemed to resonate with a deep, unsettling feeling in Elias's gut, echoing the visions that had haunted him since he first discovered the locket. "The island itself is a nexus of dark energy," Brother Thomas continued. "It amplifies the power of the blood moon, creating a perfect conduit for Morwen's dark magic."

"And the sacrifices?" Ragnar's spectral voice rumbled, his words resonating with a chilling intensity. "What does she require?"

Brother Thomas hesitated, his gaze fixed on the map. "The texts speak of a 'blood sacrifice,' a ritual offering of immense power," he explained slowly. "But the details are scarce, shrouded in cryptic symbols and ambiguous phrasing. We believe she requires not just any sacrifice, but one infused with... potent magic."

Leif, ever the strategist, leaned forward. "Potent magic? What kind?"

"The texts hint at a lineage," Brother Thomas replied, his eyes gleaming with a disturbing realization. "A line of sorcerers, descended from a powerful ancient bloodline, each possessing a unique magical affinity. Their life force, their essence, amplified by the blood moon ritual, would unlock the gateway to unleashing...him."

"Him?" Ivar's spectral form shifted, a hint of unease in his silent presence. The very air seemed to grow colder at the implication of the unspeakable being they were now dealing with.

"A being of unimaginable power," Brother Thomas confirmed, a shiver running down his spine. "A demon warlord, imprisoned centuries ago. His name is lost to time, but the consequences of his release are well documented – utter devastation, the end of the known world as we know it."

The information hung in the air, heavy and suffocating. The weight of responsibility pressed down on Elias, the spectral warriors echoing his silent dread. The training, the grueling exercises, the relentless pressure from the Silver Eagles – it had all prepared them for combat, but this... this was something else entirely. This was a fight against forces beyond comprehension, against a threat that transcended mere physical strength.

Bjorn, ever the pragmatist, broke the silence. "So, we need to stop her before the blood moon rises," he stated, his voice resolute. "We need to get to Cairn of Whispers and prevent the ritual."

Hroar, his spectral form barely visible in the shadows, added, "But how? How do we infiltrate a sorceress's lair, knowing she's prepared for us?"

It was Leif who answered. "We need a plan. A well-constructed plan, utilizing all our resources and abilities. The Silver Eagles' training has given us a tactical advantage, but we still need to understand Morwen's strengths and weaknesses. We need intelligence, a way in without being noticed."

They spent the next few days poring over ancient texts, deciphering cryptic clues, piecing together fragments of information. They learned about Morwen's methods, her past, her alliances. They uncovered hidden passages within the monastery's library, uncovering forgotten prophecies and diagrams of magical artifacts.

They learned that Morwen had gathered a powerful army of mercenaries, dark mages, and creatures of nightmare, creatures born from the deepest shadows. They were far from alone in their opposition to Morwen's plan. Word had spread of her dark ambition, and a coalition of resistance began to form.

The monks provided them with ancient maps, detailing secret passages and hidden entrances to Cairn of Whispers. They were led to a hidden chamber where an old scroll, protected for generations, revealed the layout of Morwen's lair. The scroll was intricately detailed, showing defensive structures, patrols, and magical barriers that guarded the ritual site. They deciphered the precise timings of the various stages of the ritual, and learned about Morwen's use of enchanted wards and protective enchantments.

The mercenaries, on the other hand, contributed their practical battlefield experience. They analyzed the scroll's information and developed various infiltration strategies, taking into account the terrain, the enemy's movements, and the possibility of encountering magical traps. They developed contingencies for various scenarios: ambushes, unexpected reinforcements, and even a potential betrayal within their own ranks. They discussed weapons and equipment, adapting their supplies to meet the unique challenges presented by the island's environment and Morwen's supernatural defenses. They considered the use of magical countermeasures, relying on their combined knowledge to counteract Morwen's spells.

The mercenaries suggested using cloaking spells and distraction tactics to bypass the protective enchantments. They also discussed the possibility of using strategic alliances with other factions who opposed Morwen's rule.

From the monks, they gained a deeper understanding of Morwen's motivations, her past, and her vulnerabilities. They learned about the specific type of magical energy she drew upon, her weaknesses to certain types of magical attacks, and her reliance on specific rituals for maintaining her power. They also learned that Morwen was not completely invincible, and that certain spells and artifacts could weaken her considerably. This knowledge was crucial in the development of their strategy. They learned about Morwen's obsessive pursuit of power, her willingness to sacrifice anything to achieve her goals, and her deep-seated hatred of those who stood in her way.

As the blood moon loomed closer, casting an eerie glow over the landscape, Elias and his companions finalized their plans. They were prepared to face any challenge, for they knew that failure would mean the end of everything they held dear. They had the knowledge, the skills, and the unity of purpose to stand against a darkness that threatened to consume the world. The path ahead remained perilous, but their resolve was unshaken. They would stop Morwen, no matter the cost. The fate of the world rested on their shoulders, and they were ready to bear the burden.

The relentless training regimen imposed by the Silver Eagles had forged a bond amongst them stronger than any forged in fire. Elias, once a solitary outcast, now found himself inextricably linked to the spectral Vikings and the seasoned mercenaries. Their shared near-death experiences, the grueling physical and mental trials they endured together, had created an unbreakable brotherhood, a unity of purpose that transcended the boundaries of life and death.

The bond between Elias and the Viking spirits was particularly profound. He had initially been their unwilling vessel, a conduit for their resurrected power. But as days bled into nights, the line between them blurred. He felt their rage, their sorrow, their ancient wisdom coursing through his veins. He learned their battle cries, their strategies, their unwavering loyalty to one another, a legacy that echoed across the centuries. Ragnar, the fierce and unwavering leader, instilled in Elias a sense of unwavering determination. Bjorn, the pragmatic strategist, taught him the importance of planning and foresight. Leif, the cunning tactician, sharpened his wit and tactical prowess. Hroar, the silent observer, helped him to develop a deeper understanding of his surroundings and anticipate his opponent's moves. Ivar, the enigmatic warrior, opened Elias's mind to unconventional solutions and strategies, fostering an adaptability he never possessed before. Their experiences were interwoven, their memories shared, forming a powerful tapestry of shared history and mutual respect.

The mercenaries, hardened by years of brutal warfare, initially viewed the spectral Vikings with suspicion and skepticism. Yet, as they witnessed the Vikings' unwavering loyalty and the depth of Elias's connection to them, their reservations gradually melted away. The mercenaries, initially skeptical of Elias's abilities, were impressed by his resilience and courage in battle. They recognized his natural leadership qualities, his ability to inspire and motivate his allies, even in the face of overwhelming odds. His training under the Silver Eagles, combined with the Vikings' ancient fighting techniques and strategies, had made him a formidable opponent. He was no longer just an ordinary boy; he was a warrior, a leader, a force to be reckoned with.

The shared nights spent huddled around flickering campfires, sharing stories and strategies, strengthened their bonds. They discussed the intricacies of Morwen's power, analyzing her weaknesses and predicting her moves. They planned their attack on Cairn of Whispers, each contributing their unique skills and expertise. The Vikings shared their ancient knowledge of magic and warfare, passing down their wisdom and skills through generations.

The mercenaries contributed their battlefield experience, their knowledge of tactics and strategy. Elias, the bridge between the two worlds, translated their knowledge and ensured seamless cooperation, fostering a spirit of mutual respect and trust among his unlikely allies.

One evening, as the wind howled outside their temporary shelter, Elias found himself sharing a quiet moment with Ragnar. The spectral warrior, usually a picture of stoic strength, showed a rare vulnerability. "We failed once, Elias," Ragnar said, his spectral voice low and mournful. "We failed to protect our people. We will not fail again."

Elias met Ragnar's gaze. "We won't," he replied firmly. "We're not them. We're stronger, together." He felt a surge of power, a shared determination, flowing between them, a strength drawn not just from the Viking spirits but from the shared trials and triumphs they had endured together.

The bond between Elias and the mercenaries deepened in the crucible of shared danger. They faced ambushes, navigating treacherous terrain, and narrowly escaping deadly magical traps set by Morwen's forces. During one particularly harrowing encounter, a mercenary, Ronan, was severely injured protecting Elias from a monstrous creature summoned by Morwen. The Vikings, despite their ethereal forms, risked their spectral essence to heal Ronan, demonstrating a selfless dedication to their human allies. Elias felt a surge of gratitude and shared grief as he witnessed the camaraderie between his human and spectral companions. This act of selfless sacrifice transcended their differences and solidified their bond.

The trust they developed was absolute. They relied on each other implicitly, their combined strength far greater than the sum of their individual parts. Elias's strategic insights, honed by the Vikings' wisdom and the mercenaries' experience, allowed them to overcome obstacles they never could have faced alone. They adapted their strategies on the fly, anticipating their opponent's moves, reacting quickly and effectively to the unexpected. They became a finely tuned fighting machine, a cohesive unit that moved with precision and deadly efficiency.

The shared threat of Morwen unified them. Their differences—the clash of ancient Viking culture and modern mercenary practicality, the spectral nature of the Vikings versus the tangible reality of the mercenaries, and Elias's position as the bridge between these worlds—paled in comparison to the overwhelming danger they faced. They understood that their survival depended on their unity and their ability to overcome their individual differences to fight as one.

The upcoming blood moon ritual loomed over them, a palpable threat that bound them closer together. The pressure of impending doom fostered a sense of urgency and desperation, forcing them to overcome any remaining doubts or suspicions. They knew that only by working together, by relying on each other completely, could they hope to defeat Morwen and prevent the release of the demon warlord. This shared sense of danger and the weight of responsibility served as a powerful catalyst for forging their unbreakable bond.

Their differences, once a source of potential conflict, became their greatest strength. The Vikings provided unparalleled knowledge of ancient magic and warfare, while the mercenaries brought their battlefield experience and tactical prowess. Elias, the unlikely leader, bridged the gap between them, harnessing their combined strengths to create a formidable fighting force. They learned to trust each other's instincts, anticipating each other's moves, and reacting as a single unit in the face of danger. Their combined strength was more than the sum of their parts; it was a synergy of skills and experience forged in the fires of shared adversity. This wasn't just a battle for survival, but a testament to the strength of their bond, a testament to what they could achieve when they put aside their differences and fought together as one.

As the blood moon hung heavy in the sky, casting an ominous glow over their preparations, they stood ready, united in their purpose, ready to face any challenge that lay ahead. Their bond, forged in the fires of adversity, was their greatest weapon, a force that would prove more potent than any spell or sword.

The air crackled with an unnatural energy, a tangible sense of dread that pressed down on them like a physical weight. The blood moon, a malevolent crimson orb, hung heavy in the sky, its ominous glow casting long, distorted shadows across the landscape. Time, Elias knew, was their most formidable enemy. Every passing moment brought Morwen closer to achieving her dark ritual, every second ticked away like grains of sand in an hourglass that measured the fate of the kingdom, perhaps even the world.

Their journey towards Cairn of Whispers, the ancient, forgotten ruin where Morwen planned to perform her ritual, was fraught with peril. The path itself seemed to conspire against them, twisting and turning through a labyrinth of treacherous terrain. Jagged rocks jutted out from the earth like skeletal fingers, threatening to trip and cripple them. Dense forests, choked with gnarled trees and thorny undergrowth, slowed their progress, each step a battle against the relentless wilderness. The wind, a mournful keening in the oppressive stillness of the night, carried whispers of impending doom.

Morwen's forces, shadowy figures flitting through the darkness, were relentless in their pursuit. They were not just ordinary soldiers, but creatures warped by dark magic, their bodies twisted into grotesque parodies of humanity. Wraiths, their forms shimmering and translucent, drifted silently through the undergrowth, their spectral claws reaching out to snatch at their allies. Ghouls, their flesh rotting and decaying, lurked in the shadows, their eyes burning with unholy light, their hunger insatiable. Even the very earth seemed to be animated by Morwen's dark magic, twisting into monstrous shapes, attempting to ensnare them in its grasp.

The Vikings, despite their ethereal nature, were not immune to fatigue. The constant strain of battling Morwen's forces, the sheer exhaustion of maintaining their spectral forms, visibly weakened them. Ragnar, normally a bulwark of strength, occasionally stumbled, his spectral form flickering, his breath ragged, a stark

reminder of their precarious situation. The burden of their past, the weight of their failed defense, rested heavily upon them, a silent pressure that added to the physical exhaustion.

The mercenaries, though hardened veterans of countless battles, showed signs of strain. Their faces, etched with exhaustion and worry, mirrored the grim reality of their situation. Ronan, still recovering from his injuries, moved with a stiff gait, his every movement a testament to the pain he endured. His unwavering loyalty and commitment to their cause remained, but the physical toll was undeniable. Yet, their experience and their loyalty to Elias and their shared cause pushed them forward. Their combined expertise, their unwavering determination, were their greatest weapons.

Elias, the unlikely leader, felt the weight of responsibility crushing him. He was not only a warrior, but a strategist, a navigator, a healer – he was the linchpin of their fragile alliance. He relied on the wisdom of the Vikings and the experience of the mercenaries, but it was his resolve that kept them moving forward, his leadership that inspired them to face the challenges that lay ahead. He was no longer the outcast boy; he was their leader, their protector, their hope.

Their progress was slow, agonizingly so. Each step forward was met with resistance, each victory a hard-fought battle. But they pressed on, driven by a shared purpose, bound together by a bond stronger than any magic, fueled by a desperate hope that they might somehow succeed. The blood moon's crimson light cast an eerie glow upon their faces, highlighting the grim determination etched into their features.

One night, as they sought refuge in a crumbling stone edifice, a sudden storm descended upon them. The wind howled like a tormented beast, lashing rain against the stone walls, blurring their vision and obscuring their path. Lightning illuminated the landscape, revealing the terrifying scale of Morwen's forces that surrounded them. The mercenaries huddled together, their shields raised, forming a protective barrier against the relentless assault. The Vikings, their spectral forms shimmering in the flashes of lightning, fought with a ferocity that transcended their ethereal existence.

Elias, using his newfound knowledge of ancient runes, channeled the energy of the storm, unleashing a powerful blast of wind and lightning that scattered Morwen's forces, buying them precious time to regroup and escape. But even as they celebrated their temporary reprieve, a chilling realization dawned upon them - Morwen was stronger than they anticipated, her forces seemingly limitless.

They were outnumbered, outmatched, and out of time. Yet, the shared fear fueled their resolve. They were facing not only physical threats but also the relentless erosion of their hopes. The doubt gnawed at the edges of their determination, especially among the mercenaries who, unlike the Vikings, were mortal and vulnerable.

Elias sensed their wavering and knew that his role wasn't just leading them in battle but in maintaining their morale and preventing their dwindling hope from collapsing completely. He shared stories of their victories, of the bond they had forged, reminding them of their shared strength. He focused on what they could control – their actions in the present – instead of allowing the looming blood moon and Morwen's ever-growing forces to cripple their spirits.

As dawn approached, painting the sky with streaks of pale light, they emerged from their temporary refuge, weary but unbroken. The Cairn of Whispers was in sight, its ominous silhouette looming against the blood-red horizon. The final battle was upon them, a desperate race against time, a struggle for survival that would determine the fate of their world. They pressed onward, their steps heavy, their hearts filled with a mixture of fear, determination, and unwavering loyalty to one another, their bond strengthened by the trials they had endured. The looming shadow of the blood moon, once a symbol of dread, now served as a reminder of the shared destiny that bound them together—a reminder of the fight they had to win. They were not just fighting for survival, they were fighting for a future worth living for, a future secured through their unity and unwavering hope. The race against time had brought them to the brink, but it was in this very precipice that their strength would be truly tested, and their bond would be forged unbreakably in the crucible of the impending battle.

The deceptive calm of the pre-dawn hours shattered with the shriek of a warhorn, a sound that ripped through the fragile peace they had managed to salvage. From the shadows of the whispering pines, a tide of Morwen's forces surged forth, their numbers seemingly limitless, their ferocity relentless. This was no mere patrol; this was a full-scale assault, orchestrated with a precision that spoke of meticulous planning, a chilling testament to Morwen's cunning.

As Elias adjusted his grip on his sword, he felt a new sensation ripple through his chest — a presence both powerful and unfamiliar. A sixth voice, calm but commanding, echoed in his mind.

"You've finally proven worthy of my strength," the voice said. *"I am Astrid, shieldmaiden and rune-weaver. I watched in silence while the others guided you. But now, with the tide turning, I see the fire in your heart. You're ready."*

Elias blinked, staggered by the intensity of her arrival. The others remained silent, as if acknowledging what her emergence meant — a new bond, forged not by force, but by choice.

The initial onslaught was brutal, a whirlwind of steel and dark magic. The mercenaries, their formations already strained from their previous battles, struggled to hold the line. Ronan, his wounds still raw, fought with a grim determination, his blade a blur of motion, deflecting blows that would have felled lesser men. His lieutenant, Kael, a seasoned warrior with a grim face and eyes that reflected the harsh realities of countless battles, roared orders, his voice a counterpoint to the cacophony of clashing steel. But even their skill and experience could not withstand the sheer weight of Morwen's army.

The Vikings, spectral as they were, fought with a terrifying efficiency. Their ethereal forms shimmered and flickered as they moved through the ranks of Morwen's soldiers, their ghostly blades leaving trails of stunned and dying enemies in their wake. Ragnar, despite his weakening form, fought like a berserker, his spectral fury a terrifying spectacle. Bjorn and Astrid, their movements swift and deadly, carved paths through the enemy ranks, their ghostly presence a harbinger of death. But the sheer number of Morwen's forces was relentless, the unrelenting pressure threatening to overwhelm them.

Elias, caught in the midst of the chaos, fought with the desperate courage of a cornered animal. His newfound strength, amplified by the Viking spirits, allowed him to cut through enemies, but his position was precarious. The ground beneath his feet trembled with the force of the battle, the air thick with the smell of blood and the stench of decay. He fought to maintain his focus, coordinating their defenses, his eyes constantly scanning for opportunities, for weaknesses in the enemy lines. He knew that their survival depended not just on brute strength but on strategy, on coordination, on the ability to adapt to the ever-changing tide of battle.

The ambush effectively scattered their ranks. Elias, separated from the main force, found himself facing a group of particularly formidable foes – hulking creatures, their flesh warped and contorted by dark magic, their movements jerky and unnatural. Their eyes burned with an unholy light, and their guttural roars echoed through the forest. He fought back-to-back with one of the mercenaries, a grizzled veteran named Gareth, whose experience proved invaluable in navigating the chaotic melee. Gareth, a mountain of a man with a surprisingly agile swordsmanship, provided Elias with a solid shield against the monstrous attackers, allowing Elias to unleash powerful blows that only his enhanced strength could deliver.

As the battle raged around him, Elias noticed something unsettling. Among the enemy ranks, he spotted a figure familiar, a shadow he recognized from the past. It was Kael, Elias's friend, the lieutenant of the mercenaries, his face twisted in a horrifying grimace. He seemed to be fighting with an almost unnatural ferocity, an almost obsessive focus on killing his own allies. Elias's heart lurched. The reality hit him with brutal force: Kael had been betrayed. He had been corrupted.

The realization was a chilling blow, a betrayal that struck deeper than any physical wound. Kael, a man known for his unwavering loyalty and unwavering courage, a man who had fought alongside them since their journey began, had turned against them. The doubt and fear that had been brewing on the fringes of the mercenary's minds now erupted with fierce force, threatening to dissolve their hard-earned unity.

The news spread like wildfire, striking a blow to their morale and undermining their already precarious position. The mercenaries, already exhausted and outnumbered, began to waver. Doubt and despair crept into their hearts, casting a shadow on their resolve and their ability to fight effectively. The Vikings, though untouched by such human emotions, sensed the shift in momentum, their spectral forms flickering with unease. Elias struggled to rally his remaining forces, to maintain their unity and to rekindle their spirit amidst this crisis. The betrayal was a turning point, not just militarily, but also psychologically. Their shared cause, the shared destiny that had bound them together, was being unravelled by treachery from within.

The fight continued, but it was no longer a fair battle. It was a desperate struggle for survival against a superior enemy, further complicated by the presence of a traitor within their ranks. Elias, using his new abilities, channeled his own rage into a storm of mystic energy, creating a momentary distraction that allowed some of the mercenaries to escape the immediate chaos. He had to save them, not only to preserve their strength, but also to prevent the betrayal from completely crippling their morale. The betrayal had cast a long, dark shadow over their battle. The uncertainty of who they could trust, even the possibility of other hidden traitors within their ranks, intensified the gravity of their situation.

Meanwhile, the remaining Vikings fought desperately, their ghostly forms creating momentary mayhem among the enemy ranks, but their strength was waning. Ragnar, wounded and exhausted, collapsed, his spectral form flickering dangerously. Elias rushed to his side, feeling a pang of helplessness and a renewed determination to end this nightmarish ambush. He knew that losing even one of the Vikings would be a devastating blow, not only to their fighting capacity but also to their collective morale.

As the night wore on, the chaos reached a fever pitch. The forest, once a sanctuary, became a battleground, a scene of brutal conflict and unrelenting carnage. The once-unified force was now fragmented, scattering across the landscape. Each small pocket of resistance struggled against a seemingly endless tide of Morwen's forces. Elias had to maintain hope, to find a strategy that would overcome their numerical disadvantage and ultimately defeat the traitor within their ranks.

The relentless assault showed no sign of letting up. As the blood moon climbed higher in the sky, its crimson light illuminating the carnage, the grim reality of their situation became painfully clear. They were outnumbered, outmaneuvered, and betrayed. Their carefully constructed alliance was shattered, their ranks decimated, their hope dwindling with every passing moment. Yet, even in this abyss of despair, a flicker of determination remained, a refusal to surrender, a desperate clinging to the shared purpose that had brought them together.

The battle raged on, a testament to their indomitable spirit. They fought for each other, for the future, for the world that hung in the balance, their unity severely tested, but their resolve unbroken. The night, stained red with blood and betrayal, promised to be long and bloody, a battle for survival in the face of overwhelming odds. The blood moon, a silent, malevolent witness, hung high above them, a harbinger of the trials that lay ahead.

The crimson glow of the blood moon cast long, skeletal shadows across the ravaged battlefield, painting the scene in a macabre light. The air, thick with the coppery tang of blood and the acrid stench of burnt flesh, hung heavy in Elias's lungs. He stumbled, his legs heavy with exhaustion, his body screaming in protest against the relentless onslaught. The spectral forms of the Vikings flickered weakly beside him, their power visibly waning. Ragnar, his ethereal body almost transparent, lay slumped against a gnarled tree trunk, his ghostly breaths shallow and ragged.

Elias knelt beside him, his heart aching with a helplessness he had never known. He had felt the sting of loss before, the bite of betrayal, but this was different. This was a gnawing fear that reached into the very core of his being, a doubt that threatened to unravel everything he had fought for. He looked around at the decimated ranks of the mercenaries, the few survivors huddled together, their faces etched with fear and despair. The once-proud army, a force to be reckoned with, was now a fractured, broken remnant, clinging to life by a thread.

The weight of their failure pressed down on him, crushing the spirit that had sustained him through countless battles. He had believed in their cause, in their ability to overcome Morwen's dark forces. He had believed in himself, in the strength that the Viking spirits had bestowed upon him. But now, under the malevolent gaze of the blood moon, that belief felt fragile, tenuous, ready to shatter at any moment.

A wave of self-doubt washed over him, cold and chilling. Had he been wrong? Had he been foolish to believe that he, an ordinary boy, could stand against a sorceress of Morwen's power, a woman who commanded legions of monstrous creatures and wielded magic that twisted reality itself? The spectral warriors, once a source of strength and unwavering confidence, now seemed like fragile echoes of a bygone era, their power fading, their whispers growing weaker.

He remembered the visions that had plagued him, the glimpses into the past, the horrors he had witnessed through the eyes of the fallen Vikings. He had seen their strength, their ferocity, their unwavering loyalty to one another. But he had also seen their vulnerability, their mortality, their ultimate defeat. And now, as he gazed upon the carnage around him, he couldn't shake the feeling that he was destined to repeat their mistakes.

The betrayal of Kael, his once-trusted friend and lieutenant, had struck a deeper blow than he had initially realized. It had not only weakened their forces but also shattered his faith in human loyalty, in the bonds of friendship that had seemed unbreakable. He wondered if there were other traitors amongst them, hidden in the shadows, waiting for the opportune moment to strike. The suspicion, once a faint whisper, had now grown into a deafening roar in his mind, poisoning his judgment, eroding his trust.

The thought of facing Morwen, of confronting her demonic forces, now filled him with a paralyzing terror. The weight of responsibility– the fate of the kingdom, the potential annihilation of the world – pressed down on his shoulders, threatening to crush him beneath its immense weight. He had envisioned victory, a glorious triumph over the forces of darkness. Now, he saw only defeat, an endless night of bloodshed and despair.

But even in this abyss of despair, a stubborn ember of defiance flickered within him. He looked at Ragnar, his spectral form barely visible, his breath growing weaker with each passing moment. He looked at the remaining mercenaries, their faces grim but resolute, their eyes reflecting a mixture of fear and determination. He saw their courage, their willingness to fight despite the overwhelming odds. And in that moment, he found a renewed sense of purpose, a glimmer of hope in the encroaching darkness.

He knew that he could not afford to succumb to despair. He had come too far, sacrificed too much, to let self-doubt cripple him now. He had to fight, not only for survival, but for the memory of those who had fallen, for the future of those who still lived. He had to find a way to rally his forces, to rekindle their dwindling hope, to overcome the treachery that had plagued them.

The blood moon hung heavy in the sky, its crimson light a silent witness to his internal struggle. He closed his eyes, taking a deep breath of the foul air, the metallic tang of blood filling his senses. He focused on the strength of the Viking spirits within him, on the memories of their battles, their triumphs, their defeats. He felt their rage, their sorrow, their unwavering resolve. And in that moment, he found a renewed connection to their power, a deeper understanding of their sacrifices. He realized that their strength was not just physical; it was a resilience of spirit, an unwavering commitment to a cause greater than themselves.

Opening his eyes, Elias stood up, his body aching, his spirit renewed. He might doubt his abilities, he might fear the darkness that threatened to engulf them, but he would not yield. He would fight. He would fight for his friends, for the fallen, for the world that hung precariously in the balance. This was not simply a battle for survival; it was a test of his own spirit, a crucible in which he would forge his destiny. The blood moon continued its ascent, its crimson glow casting a menacing shadow over the battlefield, but now, Elias felt a surge of defiance. The doubt was still there, a constant companion, but it no longer held him captive. He would confront his fears, face his doubts, and fight with every ounce of his renewed strength. He would find a way. He had to. The fate of the world depended on it.

He rallied the remaining mercenaries, his voice hoarse but firm, his words filled with a newfound determination. He spoke of sacrifice, of courage, of the shared responsibility that bound them together. He reminded them of the goals they had fought for, of the ideals that they held dear, of the innocent lives that depended on their victory. He spoke not of invincibility, but of resilience, of facing adversity with a united front.

He adjusted his strategy, taking into account the traitor in their ranks, the thinning numbers, and the unpredictable nature of the supernatural forces arrayed against them. He devised a plan that prioritized survival and calculated risks, a testament to his newfound strength, not just in brute force, but also in strategic thinking. He would use the forest to their advantage, utilizing the cover of darkness and the deceptive terrain to outmaneuver their larger enemy force.

The Vikings, sensing his renewed resolve, rallied alongside him, their spectral forms glowing with a renewed intensity. Ragnar, though weak, provided strategic guidance, his experience from countless battles lending invaluable insight into the enemy's tactics and weaknesses. Astrid and Bjorn, their movements quick and silent, continued to strike from unexpected angles, creating confusion and inflicting heavy casualties.

The battle continued, but the tide had begun to turn. No longer overwhelmed by despair, Elias fought with a calculated fury, using his enhanced strength and the knowledge gained from the Vikings to strategically outmaneuver the enemy, turning their numbers against them. He moved with a precision that surprised even himself, his actions informed by the combined wisdom and experiences of the five Viking warriors that lived within him. The fight was far from over, but the flickering flame of hope burned brighter, pushing back the encroaching darkness. The blood moon, still a silent witness, seemed to cast a less menacing glow, as if acknowledging the resilience of the underdog in this epic struggle. The night would continue to be a test of their will, their courage, and their unity; but now, fueled by a renewed purpose and a spirit unbroken, they were fighting not just for survival, but for a chance to reclaim a future once lost in the shadows. The battle raged on, under the crimson gaze of the blood moon, a battle that would define not only their fates, but the fate of the world itself.

The forest floor, slick with mud and blood, offered little comfort. Elias, leaning against the rough bark of an ancient oak, felt the chill seep into his bones, a coldness that went deeper than the night's damp. The weight of the dead, both human and spectral, pressed heavily on his soul. He closed his eyes, the images of the fallen Vikings, their ghostly forms fading into the darkness, replaying in his mind. Ragnar's final breath, a whisper lost to the wind, echoed in his ears.

He had failed. Or so it seemed. The initial surge of renewed determination, that fleeting moment of defiance under the blood moon's gaze, had waned, leaving him with a gnawing emptiness. The victory he had envisioned, the triumphant clash against Morwen's forces, had dissolved into a bitter retreat, a desperate scramble for survival. Kael's betrayal still stung, a wound that refused to heal, poisoning his trust in those he once held dear.

He opened his eyes, focusing on the small, flickering fire that Astrid had painstakingly managed to keep alive. Its weak light danced on the faces of the remaining mercenaries, etched with exhaustion and fear. Their silence was more deafening than any battle cry. The hope he had tried to ignite, the spark of defiance he'd attempted to kindle, seemed to have been snuffed out by the harsh reality of their situation.

Then, he remembered something Ragnar had said, a fleeting whisper from his fading spectral form: "Strength is not merely in the swing of the axe, boy, but in the spirit that wields it. It's in the bond between warriors, in the loyalty that binds them." Ragnar's words, initially dismissed as the ramblings of a dying spirit, now resonated with a clarity that startled him.

He looked at Astrid, her face smudged with dirt and blood, but her eyes bright with unwavering determination. She was tending to Bjorn's wounds, her movements precise and efficient. He saw Bjorn, his face pale, his body bruised, yet his spirit unbroken. He watched Leif and Sven, their expressions grim, but their stances resolute.

They were weary, battered, but not broken. They had lost comrades, faced overwhelming odds, and still, they stood.

And then, he looked at himself. He was weary, his body ached, his spirit bruised. But he was alive. He had felt the power of the Vikings, their strength flowing through him, giving him the ability to fight, to endure, to survive. He had experienced their memories, their battles, their triumphs, their defeats, but more importantly, he had witnessed their unwavering loyalty to one another, their fierce brotherhood, their relentless pursuit of what they believed in.

That loyalty, that brotherhood, was what had given them strength in life, and what continued to sustain them in death. It was that bond which had propelled them through countless battles, that had given them the will to fight even when faced with insurmountable odds. It was that shared purpose that had shaped their destiny, and it was that same spirit that he, Elias, now possessed.

He remembered the whispers of the Vikings, their shared memories, their collective strength. He had felt their rage, their sorrow, their unwavering commitment to their cause. He had doubted himself, doubted their strength, doubted the possibility of victory. But now, he saw that their power resided not only in their physical prowess but in their unwavering spirit, in their unbreakable bonds. He had to channel that power, that spirit, that loyalty within himself and his remaining companions.

He rose, his body stiff, but his spirit renewed. He approached Astrid, offering a hand. "We're not defeated," he said, his voice hoarse but firm. "We're wounded, yes, but we're not broken. We still have each other."

Astrid met his gaze, a flicker of understanding passing between them. She nodded, a silent acknowledgment of his renewed resolve. She looked to the others, and a quiet sense of solidarity spread through their ranks.

Elias didn't offer a grand speech, a rallying cry to inspire. He simply spoke of survival, of cooperation, of mutual support. He spoke of trust, of faith in their shared abilities. He spoke of adapting their strategy, of using their diminished numbers to their advantage. He spoke of learning from the mistakes made, of avoiding the traps that had led to their losses. He spoke of utilizing the darkness of the forest, the terrain, the elements to their advantage. He spoke of drawing on their combined skills, their individual strengths, to overcome the challenges they faced.

The fire, now stoked and growing stronger, seemed to reflect the renewed flame of hope within their ranks. The whispers of the Viking spirits were now clearer, sharper, more focused. Their collective memory offered insights into Morwen's tactics, her weaknesses, her patterns. They were not just echoes of the past; they were guides, advisors, an integral part of their present struggle.

Elias knew the road ahead would be long and arduous. They were outnumbered, outmatched, and betrayed. But he also knew they had something Morwen lacked: a shared loyalty, an unshakeable bond of trust, a combined strength that stemmed not just from physical prowess, but from the unwavering spirit of warriors, both living and spectral. They were fighting not just for survival, but for the preservation of that spirit, that bond, that legacy. The blood moon, still hanging heavy in the sky, no longer seemed a harbinger of doom, but a silent testament to their resilience, their courage, and their unyielding determination. Under its crimson gaze, they would fight, not just for their own lives, but for the future they hoped to carve out of the ashes of their past defeats. The fight was far from over, but now, they were fighting with renewed purpose, united in their cause, ready to face whatever darkness lay ahead. Their journey towards rediscovering their strength was not a linear path, but rather a constant evolution, a forging in the fires of adversity. And under the watchful eye of the blood moon, they would forge their destiny, together.

The air hung heavy with the scent of pine and damp earth, a stark contrast to the metallic tang of blood that still clung to Elias's clothes. He sat amongst the remnants of their makeshift camp, the dying embers of the fire casting long, dancing shadows that mimicked the restless spirits of the fallen Vikings. Their whispered voices, once a cacophony of fragmented memories, had begun to coalesce, forming a clearer picture of Morwen's plans and the impending ritual. The information was fragmentary, like shards of a broken mirror, but piecing them together was paramount to their survival.

Astrid, ever practical, was meticulously cleaning and sharpening their remaining weapons. Her movements were economical, precise, revealing a level of expertise honed through years of harsh experience. Bjorn, despite his injuries, was assisting her, his pale face set in a grim determination that belied his pain. Leif and Sven, their faces grim, were meticulously checking their equipment, ensuring every strap was secure, every blade honed to its deadliest edge.

While the others sharpened blades and reinforced their gear, Alistair quietly documented the terrain in a faded sketchbook. "History is written in blood and ash," he said softly, not expecting anyone to hear. "And if we survive this... someone must remember how it happened."

Finn had been unusually quiet over the past few days, often keeping to the fringes of the group, muttering to himself while scrawling diagrams in his worn notebook. Unknown to the others, he had been working tirelessly on a device he called a rune amplifier — a compact, metallic construct infused with etchings from both Viking runes and salvaged arcane circuitry. Its purpose: to stabilize and enhance the energy flow within the locket, which had begun pulsing erratically as the group neared the battlefield. Without warning, Finn stepped forward and knelt beside Elias, his fingers deftly attaching the amplifier to the locket's core. With a flick of his wrist, the runes flared to life. "It should hold now," he said, his voice tight with concentration. "Just... don't overload it again."

Elias, drawing on the collective memory of the Vikings, began to sketch a rough map of the terrain leading to the ritual site on a scrap of parchment. The blood moon, a malevolent eye in the inky sky, cast an eerie glow on the forest, illuminating the treacherous path ahead. The map was incomplete, riddled with question marks and uncertain routes, but it offered a framework for their approach.

"The path is treacherous," Leif murmured, his voice low and gravelly." Morwen has laid many traps. The old paths are booby-trapped, the rivers are infested with creatures of nightmare." His words hung in the air, unspoken anxieties hanging in the silence. The weight of their losses, the grim reality of their situation, pressed down on them. They were outnumbered, outmatched, and facing an enemy who wielded dark magic. Yet, a strange calmness settled over them; they were not merely clinging to survival; they were preparing for a fight.

"We cannot avoid the traps," Elias said, his voice firm, drawing upon Ragnar's strength. "We must anticipate them, anticipate Morwen's thinking. We need to use the forest itself as a weapon."He pointed to a section of the map. "This area, according to Ragnar's memories, is a natural chokepoint. We can use the terrain to funnel her forces, creating an advantage for us."

Sven, a master of stealth and deception, chimed in. "We can use the darkness to our advantage. If we remain unseen, we can pick off her scouts, weaken her ranks before the main assault." His plan was a deadly whisper of shadow and silence, a symphony of shadows and subtle movements.

Bjorn, despite his pain, offered a grim assessment of their own weakness. "Our numbers are greatly reduced. We lack the brute force to overwhelm her army head-on." His honesty was as valuable as the Viking's collective experience.

"We don't need brute force," Astrid countered, her voice sharp and clear. "We need strategy, precision, and the element of surprise. We use our combined skills to our advantage. Elias's knowledge of the terrain, Sven's skills in stealth, Leif's archery, my knowledge of poisons, and

Bjorn's brute strength when it's needed." Her calm confidence was infectious.

Elias nodded, tracing the outline of the ritual site on the map. "The ritual is scheduled for the peak of the blood moon," he explained, his voice gaining strength with each word. "According to the Vikings' memories, Morwen needs a specific alignment of the stars, a convergence of dark energies. We have to disrupt the ritual before it's complete. Delaying her isn't enough; we must stop her." He highlighted a strategic point near the ritual site on the map. "This point offers a good vantage point for an ambush. We can take out key members of her forces before they are positioned and ready."

The weight of responsibility settled heavily on Elias's shoulders. He was no longer just a vessel for the Viking spirits; he was their leader, their strategist, their guide. He was drawing upon their strength, their knowledge, their unwavering loyalty to each other.

They spent the remaining hours meticulously planning their strategy, dividing their tasks, and honing their approach. They practiced their maneuvers, their movements becoming more fluid, their coordination seamless. The flickering firelight painted their faces with an aura of grim determination. They were a unit, a tightly knit force, forged in the crucible of adversity, their spirit unwavering in their shared purpose. The fear of the blood moon's power had faded; they were preparing themselves to face the darkness with the shared strength of the Vikings, and the bond that had formed between them.

The hours crawled by, each one loaded with anticipation, with the threat of the coming battle. They prepared their equipment, sharpened their weapons, and reviewed their plan. Each item had been checked multiple times, but the meticulousness was a way of combating the gnawing fear that haunted them. It was a ritual in itself, a way of reclaiming control in the face of overwhelming odds. They spoke little, the unspoken words hanging heavy in the air –words of shared determination, of mutual support, of the bonds that had forged them together.

As the group finalized their preparations for the confrontation ahead, Professor Alistair lingered near the edge of the clearing, staring down at a worn leather journal cradled in his hands. His brow furrowed with concern, not fear — but urgency.

"These runes..." he muttered, eyes scanning a fragment he had tucked into the back of the book. "There's more to them. Layers of intent buried beneath the curse. I've seen something like this once before, in the archives beneath Eldholt."

He turned to Elias, his gaze heavy with meaning. "You don't need me for this battle. But the knowledge I carry — the maps, the interpretations — someone must ensure it survives. I'm going to the Eldholt vaults. If the seals there weaken... we'll need what's inside."

Elias hesitated, then nodded. "We'll hold the front line. You guard the past."

Alistair smiled faintly, closed the journal, and disappeared down the northern path. A chronicler returning to his pages.

As the blood moon rose, casting its crimson glow upon the forest, Elias felt the spirits of the Vikings surge within him, their power invigorating, their presence a source of strength and reassurance. He looked at his companions, their faces etched with a mixture of fear and determination, and felt a surge of pride. They were not just a band of mercenaries; they were a brotherhood, forged in the fires of adversity, united by a shared cause, and determined to face the darkness ahead. They were ready. The final preparations were complete. The battle for their survival, for the fate of the kingdom, was about to begin. Under the crimson gaze of the blood moon, their destiny awaited. Their final stand, against a sorceress and her demonic legion, was about to commence. The weight of the world, quite literally, rested upon their shoulders. They were ready. Or, as ready as they could possibly be.

The forest floor grew uneven underfoot as they approached the ritual site, the familiar crunch of twigs and leaves replaced by a disconcerting softness, as if they trod upon a thick carpet of moss and decaying vegetation. A chill, deeper than the night's cold, permeated the air, a palpable sense of dread that settled on their hearts like a shroud. The trees, gnarled and ancient, seemed to lean in, their branches like skeletal fingers reaching out to grasp them. The air itself thrummed with an unnatural energy, a potent pulse of dark magic that vibrated against their skin. This was no ordinary forest; this was a place of power, a nexus of ancient energies, steeped in centuries of forgotten rituals and spilled blood.

Elias, drawing on Ragnar's memories, recognized the location instantly. The ancient stones, half-buried in the earth, formed a crude circle, the remnants of a forgotten temple, its purpose now twisted and corrupted by Morwen's malevolent intent. Runes, etched deep into the stones, pulsed with a sinister light, their ancient script twisting and shifting before their eyes, whispering secrets they couldn't comprehend. The very ground seemed to hum with malevolent energy, a tangible sense of dread that clung to them like a second skin.

The circle wasn't merely a place; it was a living entity, radiating an oppressive aura of dark magic that pressed upon them, suffocating and terrifying. The air crackled with unseen energies, a tangible force that threatened to overwhelm them. The scent of ozone mingled with the stench of decay, creating an atmosphere of suffocating dread. It was a place where the veil between worlds thinned, where the boundaries between reality and nightmare blurred, and the line between life and death seemed almost nonexistent.

Astrid, her face grim, examined the runes with a practiced eye. "These are not merely markings," she whispered, her voice hushed with awe and fear. "They're conduits, channels for Morwen's magic. She's amplified the site's inherent power, making it a focal point for her ritual." She touched one of the stones, and a jolt of energy shot through her, forcing her to recoil. "Powerful," she breathed, her eyes wide with a mixture of fear and fascination. "More powerful than I imagined."

Bjorn, despite his pain, stood guard, his hand resting on the hilt of his axe. His senses, heightened by the proximity to the dark magic, picked up a myriad of subtle sounds – the rustling of unseen creatures, the snap of twigs, the faintest shift in the wind. His keen Viking senses alerted him to danger, even unseen. He felt the presence of something ancient and malevolent lurking just beyond the veil of reality, a feeling that confirmed their worst fears.

Leif, his bow strung and an arrow nocked, scanned the surrounding trees, his eyes sharp and alert. He moved silently, his movements ghostlike, a master of stealth and observation. The oppressive atmosphere made him uneasy, the heavy pressure of the dark magic almost tangible. He noted multiple points of potential ambush, places where Morwen's forces could emerge, sudden attacks from hidden places in the ancient forest.

Sven, ever the shadow, melted into the darkness, his presence barely perceptible. He was the eyes and ears of their group, a silent guardian, moving unseen, reporting back his observations through subtle gestures and whispered words. His uncanny ability to disappear into the shadows made him their most valuable asset in this treacherous terrain, a silent guardian against the overwhelming darkness.

Elias, drawing on the combined memories of the Vikings, pieced together the puzzle of the ritual site. The circle was not merely a place of power; it was a key, a lock, and a conduit. It was a gateway, a portal through which Morwen intended to unleash her demonic warlord upon the world. He pointed to a particular stone, its surface etched with a particularly intricate rune. "This is the keystone," he announced, his voice low and steady. "Disrupting this rune will disrupt the ritual."

As they moved closer to the center of the circle, the intensity of the dark magic increased. The air shimmered with unseen energies, and the ground vibrated beneath their feet. The runes pulsed with an ominous light, casting eerie shadows that danced and writhed like living things. The very air seemed to crackle with anticipation, a palpable sense of impending doom hanging heavy in the air.

They had prepared for battle, but nothing could have prepared them for the sheer power of the ritual site. It was a place of ancient evil, a place where the boundaries of reality itself seemed to crumble. The sheer concentration of dark magic made it difficult to breathe, to think, to even stand. Yet, they pressed on, driven by their determination, their loyalty, and their shared purpose. They moved like shadows through the oppressive aura. Each step was deliberate, each movement cautious, every action precise and deadly. They were ready to fight not only for themselves but for the world.

The weight of the impending confrontation pressed upon them, heavy and suffocating. They were not just facing an army; they were confronting the very essence of evil, an ancient force that threatened to consume the world. Yet, in the face of overwhelming odds, they held their ground, united by their shared purpose, their determination unwavering. They were a brotherhood, forged in the fires of adversity, bound together by fate and a shared quest to stop the darkness that had consumed their lives.

They reached the keystone, its surface pulsating with a sinister energy that sent shivers down their spines. It was a grotesque piece of power, and it pulsated with an energy that was almost palpable. Elias felt the power of the Vikings surge within him, their strength bolstering his own resolve. He raised his hand, ready to strike the keystone, to disrupt the flow of dark energy, to break the ritual before it was complete. The fate of the kingdom, and perhaps the world, rested upon his actions. The air was thick with the smell of ozone, tinged with the stench of decay and a hint of sulfur that spoke of something truly wicked and ancient.

The darkness pressed upon them, suffocating and terrifying, yet they stood firm. The moment was as heavy as the world itself. Their breaths came in ragged gasps as the unseen weight intensified, and the world itself seemed to hold its breath as they prepared to strike, a final stand against the encroaching darkness. The blood moon, high above, cast a crimson glow upon the scene, illuminating the circle of ancient stones and the determined faces of the warriors. The battle, for all the world, was about to begin.

The first wave crashed against them like a tidal surge. Not the gentle lapping of waves on a shore, but a furious onslaught of dark creatures, their forms shifting and writhing in the crimson glow of the blood moon. Grotesque things, born of shadow and nightmare, clawed and snarled, their eyes burning with malevolent intent. Some resembled twisted wolves, their fur matted with blood and grime, their howls echoing through the ancient forest. Others were humanoid, but warped and twisted, their limbs elongated and misshapen, their skin a sickly green. Still others were pure shadow, formless entities that slithered and lunged, their touch icy and chilling.

Bjorn met the first wave head-on, his axe a blur of steel, cleaving through the monstrous horde with terrifying efficiency. His roars echoed the fury of a berserker, each swing a testament to his ancient strength, each strike a brutal dance of death. The axe, imbued with the souls of countless enemies, sang a song of destruction, its blade drinking deeply of the dark creatures' blood. He fought with the savagery of a storm, a whirlwind of steel and fury, cutting a swathe through the enemy ranks.

Astrid, her staff crackling with raw magical energy, unleashed a barrage of spells. Runes blazed to life, weaving intricate patterns of power, casting bolts of searing energy that incinerated the creatures, turning them to ash and smoke. She fought with precision and grace, her movements fluid and deadly, each spell aimed with deadly accuracy. Her magic, imbued with the power of the earth, countered Morwen's darkness with its inherent strength and resilience.

Leif, a phantom in the shadows, loosed a volley of arrows. Each shot found its mark with deadly accuracy, piercing the hearts of the creatures, bringing them down with swift, efficient precision. He moved like a wraith, his movements ghostlike, silent and deadly. His bow, a weapon of unmatched lethality, was an extension of his own body, his shots as deadly as the sharp sting of a viper. He was a deadly force, precise, efficient, a warrior of stealth and lethality.

Sven, the master of shadows, weaved through the fray, his daggers flashing, silently dispatching the creatures before they could even react. He was a whirlwind of motion, a blur of steel and shadow, his strikes swift and deadly. He seemed to be everywhere and nowhere at once, a phantom dealing out death to the enemies, a silent hunter whose actions were as fluid and precise as water. His movements were like whispers in the dark, his attacks as silent and deadly as a shadow's touch.

Elias, channeling the strength of the five Vikings, found himself in the heart of the chaos. He felt the power of Ragnar's axe surging through him, adding to the power of his own blows. The memory of Ivar's cunning infused his tactical awareness, while Harald's strength amplified his blows. The combined strength was overwhelming. He moved with a speed and power he never knew he possessed, his body a vessel for ancient might. He fought not just as one man, but as five warriors, their strength and skills united within him. His blows echoed through the battle, each strike a hammer blow that smashed the monstrous creatures into pieces. His movements, fluid and precise, were like a dance of destruction.

Morwen's army was vast, a seemingly endless tide of darkness. But Elias and his allies stood firm, their determination unyielding, their resolve as strong as the mountains. They fought with the ferocity of lions, the precision of eagles, and the strength of bears. They were relentless in their attacks, their actions precise and deadly. Each strike was calculated, each movement measured. They fought back-to-back, side-by-side, a brotherhood of warriors, united against the encroaching darkness.

The battle raged for hours, a brutal and relentless clash of steel and magic, of light and shadow. The forest floor became a macabre tapestry of blood and gore, the air thick with the stench of death and decay. But Elias and his allies refused to yield. They fought with the unwavering determination of those who knew the stakes: the fate of the kingdom, and perhaps the world, rested upon their shoulders.

As the first wave retreated, a second, even more ferocious assault followed. This time, the creatures were larger, more powerful, their forms more monstrous. Among them were hulking beasts of pure muscle, their skin like iron, their claws and teeth capable of tearing through flesh and bone with ease. There were grotesque things that seemed to defy description, their forms shifting and changing, their eyes burning with a hellish light. And then, there were the wraiths, spectral beings of pure shadow, their touch capable of stealing the very life from their victims.

The battle intensified, the clash of steel against bone and magic against magic a symphony of destruction. Bjorn, his axe dripping with blood, fought with the frenzied energy of a cornered beast. Astrid's spells rained down like fire from the heavens, while Leif's arrows flew like deadly comets across the battlefield. Sven, a ghost in the darkness, flitted around the edges, silently dispatching the enemy one by one. And Elias, fueled by the combined power of the five Vikings, stood at the heart of the storm, a bastion of strength and resilience.

As the battle reached its zenith, a towering figure emerged from the ranks of Morwen's army. It was a monstrous beast, its form vaguely humanoid, but its skin was like cracked obsidian, and horns of pure bone sprouted from its skull. Its eyes burned with an infernal fire, and its roar shook the very earth. It was a creature of nightmare, a being of pure evil, and it was Morwen's champion.

This champion, an abomination created from dark magic and ancient evil, was a formidable foe, possessing strength and power far beyond that of its brethren. It swung a massive club, its blows capable of shattering stone and bone alike. It breathed blasts of fire that incinerated everything in their path, and from its body there oozed a viscous fluid that corroded the flesh.

Elias, drawing on all of his strength, engaged the beast in single combat. It was a clash of titans, a battle between good and evil, between light and darkness. The clash of their weapons echoed through the forest, the air filled with the roar of the beast and the fierce cries of Elias.

The fight was brutal and relentless, a dance of death between two powerful warriors. The beast's strength was immense, but Elias, fueled by the souls of the five Vikings, matched it blow for blow. His movements became more fluid, more powerful, his attacks more ferocious. He was not just fighting for survival; he was fighting for the world.

The battle continued, a brutal dance of death between the warriors. Each blow was a thunderclap, each parry a flash of light. The ground trembled under the weight of their clash. The air crackled with power, the magic of Elias combating the sheer brute force of the creature. The blood moon cast its crimson light upon the scene, illuminating the desperate struggle between light and darkness.

Finally, as the beast launched another mighty blow, Elias used his combined knowledge and agility, his reflexes far exceeding what he could do normally. He anticipated the attack, weaving deftly around the blow and striking with a calculated, deadly blow. The strike landed on the beast's neck, slicing through the obsidian flesh. The creature roared in pain, its body convulsing before collapsing to the ground with a resounding thud.

With the fall of the champion, the tide of battle turned. Morwen's army, demoralized and leaderless, began to retreat. Elias and his allies pressed their advantage, driving the remaining creatures into the depths of the forest. The battle ended as it began - with the relentless onslaught of good against the forces of evil, and the victory was hard-won, but certain. The forest floor was littered with the dead. But it was a necessary death, paving the way for a future that was devoid of the impending doom. The victory was hard-won, but it was victory nonetheless.

The air hung thick with the scent of blood and ozone, the silence following the brutal battle a stark contrast to the recent cacophony of death. Elias, chest heaving, leaned heavily on his makeshift spear, the combined strength of the five Vikings still thrumming beneath his skin, yet fading. The victory was pyrrhic. While Morwen's immediate forces had been routed, a deep weariness settled over him, a fatigue that went beyond physical exhaustion. He felt a gnawing emptiness, a sense of something lost, something vital.

He looked down at the locket, the artifact that had been both his salvation and his curse. It pulsed faintly against his skin, its surface cool, almost lifeless. The runes etched into its silver surface, once blazing with vibrant energy, were now dull, their luminescence dimmed. The battle had taken its toll, not just on the physical world, but on the very essence of the artifact itself.

Astrid approached cautiously, her eyes filled with concern. "Elias," she began, her voice soft, "you are... different."

He knew what she meant. The transformation, the power surge he'd experienced during the battle, had been immense. He'd felt the full weight of the five Vikings within him, their strength, their skills, their memories flooding his consciousness. It was exhilarating, terrifying, and ultimately, exhausting. But it wasn't just the physical changes. He'd felt their emotions too—the burning rage of Bjorn, the quiet determination of Leif, the cunning of Ivar, the unwavering loyalty of Harald, and Ragnar's boundless courage. It was a symphony of souls, a complex tapestry of experiences woven into the fabric of his being.

Leif, ever watchful, checked his quiver, his movements betraying a quiet unease. "The locket," he murmured, his gaze fixed on the artifact. "It's... weaker."

Sven, his usually sharp features drawn and pale, nodded in agreement. "The power it gave Elias... it came at a price." He touched the locket gently, as if hesitant to disturb its fading energy. "It felt... as if the locket itself was fighting back."

Bjorn, despite his wounds, stood tall, his demeanor stoic. "We pushed it too far. We demanded more than it could give." His voice held a hint of regret, a rare vulnerability in the fierce warrior.

The truth struck Elias with the force of a physical blow. He hadn't just been fighting Morwen's army; he'd been draining the power of the locket itself. Each surge of strength, each act of superhuman resilience, had chipped away at the artifact's inherent energy. He'd pushed it beyond its limits, forced it to sustain an expenditure far beyond its capacity. It was a desperate gamble, and he had won, but at what cost?

The locket, he now realized, wasn't merely a vessel for the Vikings' souls; it was a conduit, a source of immense, ancient power. He'd felt its strength flowing through him, but now, the flow had weakened, almost to the point of stagnation. The vibrant energy that had surged within him during the battle was now a faint whisper, a dying ember.

He touched the locket again, his fingers tracing the faded runes. He could almost feel the souls within, their strength dwindling, their energies ebbing away. He felt a deep connection to them, a bond forged in the heat of battle, but that bond was now threatened, fragile, possibly breaking.

Astrid placed a hand on his shoulder, her touch surprisingly firm. "We have to find a way to restore its power," she said, her voice filled with determination. "If the locket fails, we fail."

The weight of that statement settled heavily upon Elias. He knew the locket wasn't just a source of power; it was a key. It was the only thing standing between them and Morwen's ultimate plan—a plan that involved far more than just a simple army of monsters and wraiths. It was a plan that threatened to unleash an ancient evil upon the world, an evil that the five Vikings had fought and died to contain centuries ago.

Their immediate victory was just a small reprieve, a temporary respite before the final confrontation. Morwen would return, stronger, more desperate. Without the locket's power, they stood no chance.

"But how?" Elias asked, his voice barely a whisper. The question hung heavy in the air, unanswered, filled with the weight of their dire situation. They had won one battle, but the war was far from over. The true test was yet to come, and the stakes were higher than ever before. The fate of the world rested on their ability to restore the locket's power, a feat that seemed insurmountable.

The days that followed were a blur of frantic activity. They searched ancient texts, consulted forgotten maps, sought out forgotten lore. They sought knowledge from hermits and wise women who lived deep in the woods, seeking answers from ancient ruins in an attempt to decipher the locket's secrets. They learned of its creation, of the vengeful sorceress who had trapped the Vikings' souls, and of the immense power it contained, the immense sacrifice made in the creation of the powerful artifact.

They discovered the locket was not just a vessel, but a living entity of sorts, its power connected to ley lines, the earth's own energetic currents. Its weakness, they learned, wasn't merely due to overuse, but to a disruption in the flow of this ancient energy. Morwen, they discovered, had somehow managed to sever the locket's connection to these vital currents. It was a deliberate act, designed to weaken the Vikings' power and prepare the way for her own dark ritual.

Restoring the locket's power, therefore, wouldn't be a simple matter of recharging it. It would require a journey, a perilous quest to reconnect the artifact to the earth's energy, a journey filled with potential risks. It was a race against time, a desperate struggle to restore the balance before Morwen could complete her ritual, a ritual that would unleash a power that could shatter their world, unleashing forces beyond imagination.

They learned of a sacred site, a place of immense power located deep within the heart of a forgotten mountain range, a place where the ley lines converged, a place where the earth's energy flowed freely. It was said to be a place of great power, a nexus of magic that connected the mortal realm to something greater. If they could reach this site, if they could reconnect the locket to this powerful current, then perhaps, just perhaps, they could restore its power and, in turn, save themselves.

The journey promised to be treacherous. The mountain range was known to be haunted, filled with mythical creatures and perilous traps. It was a land of dark magic and ancient secrets, a testing ground for any who dared to tread. Morwen herself would likely be guarding this place, attempting to prevent them from restoring the locket's full capacity. Yet, the task seemed impossible, but it was the only path forward.

Their determination was unwavering, fueled by the weight of their responsibility. Elias, carrying the burden of five warriors' souls, led the way, his steps steady, his resolve strengthened by the knowledge that failure meant the end of their world. The path ahead was dark and fraught with danger, but they walked forward, united against the encroaching darkness, ready to face whatever challenges lay ahead. The final confrontation loomed, and the destiny of the world rested upon their shoulders, and the fragile power of the ancient locket.

The air grew colder, a palpable shift in the atmosphere that had nothing to do with the waning light. A low, guttural growl, barely audible at first, vibrated through the ground, resonating deep within Elias's bones. It was a sound that spoke of ancient evil, of primordial darkness unleashed. The locket, nestled against his chest, pulsed with a frantic, erratic rhythm, its faint light flickering like a dying candle flame. The runes, dull just moments ago, now glowed with an ominous crimson light, the pattern twisting and shifting, morphing into something grotesque and unfamiliar.

Astrid gasped, her hand flying to her mouth. "The demon... he's awakening," she whispered, her voice trembling.

Leif, ever vigilant, nocked an arrow, his gaze fixed on the distant horizon, where an unnatural darkness began to coalesce, a swirling vortex of shadows that seemed to consume the very light. Sven muttered a prayer in the old Norse tongue, his face etched with fear, a fear that ran deeper than simple battlefield terror. Bjorn, even with his wounds still fresh, stood firm, his grip tightening on the ancient axe at his side. But even his steely resolve seemed to waver in the face of this encroaching horror. Ragnar, always the most emotionally subdued, showed fear in his eyes that even Elias couldn't ignore. He had seen the horrors the demon was capable of, lived them through the memories he now shared.

The growl intensified, growing into a roar that shook the very foundations of the earth. The ground trembled, cracks spider-webbing across the ravaged battlefield. Trees uprooted themselves, tossed aside like flimsy toys by an unseen force. The air crackled with energy, a tangible, suffocating power that pressed down on them, threatening to crush them beneath its weight.

From the heart of the darkness, a shape began to emerge, slowly at first, then with terrifying speed. It was a colossal figure, impossibly tall, its form obscured by swirling shadows, yet hinting at a monstrous power, a malevolent presence that filled them with dread. Horns, long and curved like the tusks of a monstrous beast, pierced the darkness, and eyes burned with an infernal light, piercing the shadows, seeming to stare directly at them, reaching into their souls.

The demon warlord, Malkor, had awakened.

His presence was an overwhelming tide of pure evil, a palpable force that threatened to extinguish the very light of the world. The air itself felt corrupted, poisoned by his aura, a stench of sulfur and decay that filled their nostrils, choking them with its foulness. Elias, the combined strength of the five Vikings coursing through his veins, felt a weakness, a tremor of fear that he hadn't experienced even in the face of Morwen's wrath. This was something different, something far older and more powerful. It was the embodiment of pure, unadulterated evil.

Malkor's voice, a deafening bellow that shattered the silence, echoed across the landscape. It wasn't a human voice, but a cacophony of screams and roars, a symphony of torment and anguish. It was the sound of a thousand deaths, a chorus of suffering echoing through the ages, a testament to the untold horrors he'd inflicted throughout the centuries.

The ground beneath them buckled and cracked, fissures opening up, spewing forth plumes of black smoke and fiery embers. The air grew thick with the smell of brimstone, the taste acrid and burning in their mouths. They were surrounded by the raw, unfiltered power of pure evil, an energy so potent, so overwhelming, that it threatened to obliterate their very existence.

The Vikings within Elias stirred, their memories flooding his mind, vivid images of past battles against Malkor flashing before his eyes. He saw their desperate struggle, their valiant defense against an insurmountable foe, their eventual defeat and capture. He felt their fear, their pain, their agonizing deaths. He understood now why the locket had been created, the immense effort required to contain such a terrifying force, a force that now threatened to break free from its prison, to flood the world with its darkness.

Malkor raised a clawed hand, and a bolt of pure, black energy shot forth, streaking across the sky towards them. The ground exploded where it impacted, sending up a geyser of molten rock and fire. The heat was intense, searing their skin, yet they stood their ground, their combined strength barely holding them together, as they felt the power of the demon wash over them.

The battle was inevitable. They were vastly outnumbered, outmatched in strength and power. But they could not yield. They had come too far, sacrificed too much to falter now. The fate of the world rested on their shoulders, on their ability to defeat Malkor, to restore balance to the world.

The battle began, a chaotic maelstrom of fire and steel. Elias, fueled by the combined strength of the Vikings and the faint, fading power of the locket, fought with a ferocity born of desperation. He moved with a speed and agility he'd never possessed before, his blows landing with crushing force. He was a whirlwind of destruction, a force of nature unleashed, a warrior forged in the fires of countless battles.

Astrid, Leif, and Sven fought beside him, their skills honed by years of training and battle, their loyalty unwavering. They were a shield, protecting Elias, buying him time to use the locket's energy and unleash the full force of the Vikings' power against Malkor. They fought with unmatched courage, their movements coordinated, their actions seamless. They fought not merely for survival, but for the fate of the world. Even Bjorn, despite his severe wounds, roared as he charged at Malkor with his axe, bringing the full force of his strength and rage to bear upon the demon warlord.

But Malkor was a force of nature himself, an embodiment of raw, primordial chaos. His attacks were relentless, his power overwhelming. He struck with the force of a collapsing mountain, his attacks shattering the earth, creating craters in the very ground. His eyes gleamed with an unnatural light, and his roars seemed to crack the very fabric of reality.

The battle raged, a brutal and desperate struggle for survival. The warriors fought with a fierce determination, yet Malkor's power was far too great. They were slowly being overwhelmed. The locket's power continued to fade, threatening to leave Elias vulnerable and exposed to Malkor's wrath.

As the fight continued, Elias felt the Vikings' spirits within him weakening. Their strength was dwindling, their memories fading. The locket's connection to the ley lines, already severed by Morwen, was almost completely gone. It pulsed faintly now, a whisper of its former power. They were losing, and fast. The demon was too strong, too powerful. His very presence was destroying their world, and they were powerless to stop him.

Despite their combined strength, despite their fierce determination, Malkor began to gain the upper hand. His attacks became more powerful, his strikes more precise. Elias, Astrid, Leif, Sven, and Bjorn were being pushed back, their defenses crumbling under the relentless onslaught. The weight of the world, the burden of their responsibility, pressed down upon them, threatening to crush them.

The only hope seemed to lie in restoring the locket's power, but the sacred site where the ley lines converged was miles away, a perilous journey that seemed impossible amidst this chaos. The demon warlord was growing stronger with each passing moment, his victory seeming inevitable. The world was on the brink of collapse, and their only weapon, their only hope, was fading fast. They were trapped in a desperate fight for survival, with the fate of the world hanging precariously in the balance. The fight wasn't just against Malkor, it was a fight against time itself. And time, it seemed, was running out.

Chapter 30: Sacrifice and Loss

The earth groaned under Malkor's onslaught, fissures splitting the
ground like a shattered mirror. Each blow from the demon warlord
sent tremors through Elias's body, the combined strength of the
Vikings within him struggling against a force far beyond their
comprehension. He could feel their essence fading, their memories
dissolving like smoke in the wind. Ragnar, ever stoic, was the first to
go, his spirit whispering a farewell, a final echo of his strength leaving
Elias feeling a tangible weakening. A profound sense of loss washed
over him, a grief as vast and ancient as the demon himself. Ragnar's
strength, once a pillar supporting him, vanished, leaving a hollow ache
in his soul.

Bjorn, his body wracked with pain from both his old and new wounds,
roared a challenge, but his attack was feeble against Malkor's might.
The demon effortlessly swatted him aside like an insect, sending the
warrior crashing into a jagged rock. Elias watched in horror as Bjorn
lay still, his spirit following Ragnar into the void, leaving Elias with
another pang of grief, his strength diminishing further. The combined
power of the five Vikings was not just their collective might; it was
their indomitable spirits, their shared experiences, their unbreakable
bond. With each loss, Elias felt a piece of himself shattering, a
fragment of his own being dissolving into the void alongside them.

Astrid, her face grim with determination, launched a volley of arrows,
each tipped with a potent mixture of herbs and enchanted materials.
But even her skill proved insufficient against Malkor's overwhelming
power. The demon warlord deflected the arrows with a careless
sweep of his hand, the projectiles shattering harmlessly against an
invisible barrier of dark energy. Her spirit faltered, she felt her body
trembling. She felt the burden of her comrades' deaths weigh upon
her, a crushing weight threatening to break her. She had lost many
battles, but losing friends to the chaos was something new and painful.

Leif, ever the strategist, fought with calculated precision. His sword, imbued with runes of protection, danced like a viper, seeking weak points in Malkor's defense. But his strikes, usually so effective, were met with an impenetrable force field, the demon's power seemingly boundless. Each parry drained his energy and hope, and he felt the weight of the battle's cruelty. He desperately tried to think of a strategy that wasn't a suicide mission, yet with each passing moment their options narrowed, their hopes fading faster than the locket's light.

Sven, ever devout, continued to chant ancient Norse prayers, trying to summon the aid of forgotten gods. But even his unwavering faith seemed to be failing him, as the ground trembled with the sheer power of Malkor, and the prayers seemed lost in the cacophony of the battle. His own body and spirit screamed in pain as he felt each death of his comrades, yet he held on, his hope for survival clinging to thin air, his prayers echoing into oblivion. The weight of everything fell upon his shoulders.

The locket, its crimson light flickering weakly, pulsed with a desperate rhythm, its connection to the ley lines severed, almost beyond repair. Elias felt the final vestiges of the Vikings' strength slipping away, leaving him feeling exposed, vulnerable, alone. He was merely a vessel, now almost emptied, about to be abandoned by the souls he once contained. The overwhelming sorrow threatens to consume him, the weight of loss threatening to break him completely. He knew, with chilling certainty, that without their power, he stood no chance.

He staggered back, the last of Sven's power vanishing from his body, leaving him breathless and reeling. He was alone, facing Malkor's unrelenting might, his hope dwindling to a flicker in the darkness. He was only Elias, the outcast boy. He was not a Viking. He was mortal, and this was his end.

A fierce determination surged through him. He wouldn't let them die in vain. He would find a way, even if it meant sacrificing everything he had left. Remembering the location of the ley lines, etched in his mind through Ragnar's memories, he made his decision. He had to reach the

sacred site, even if it meant his own demise. He had to restore the locket's power, even if it meant facing Malkor alone. He had to fight, for every life lost, for the world's
survival.

Ignoring Malkor's furious attacks, Elias turned and ran, his body aching, his spirit wounded, but his resolve unbroken. He knew the journey was a suicide mission, but he had to try. He had to find a way to stop Malkor, no matter the cost. He had to find a way to bring back his friends. He had to win. He ran as fast as his legs would carry him, the demon's roars echoing behind him, like the chilling whispers of death itself. He ran through the ravaged landscape, his mind focused only on his goal, the sacred site. He ran, fueled by the memories of his fallen comrades, their sacrifices, and the shared weight of their responsibility. He ran towards his destiny, the fate of everything resting on his shoulders. He ran towards hope, the only hope left in the collapsing world.

The journey was perilous, the landscape scarred by Malkor's destructive power. He evaded falling debris, leaped over chasms, navigated through rivers of molten rock, and evaded the demon's relentless pursuit. The demon's attacks were like a storm, and he had to move at the speed of lightning to avoid certain death.

Finally, exhausted and bleeding, he reached the sacred site, a hidden clearing where the ley lines converged, pulsating with raw energy. He stumbled, his body almost giving way. He collapsed, his strength completely drained, but just enough left to activate the locket. He reached out, his trembling fingers touching the pulsing runes. A surge of power coursed through him, filling him with a strength he'd never felt before.

But it came with a price. The power surged through him, rebuilding the locket's connection to the ley lines, healing the damage caused by Morwen's attack. Yet, with the restoration of the locket's power came a surge of pain, the culmination of the sacrifices made. The memories of the Vikings flashed before his eyes, not of battle, not of glory, but of their last moments, their pain, their acceptance of their fate. Each sacrifice cemented his understanding of the true cost of victory. With renewed strength, he turned to face Malkor, but something was different. The demon warlord appeared... weakened. The light from the locket now shone brighter, stronger than ever before. Elias, fueled by the restored power and the agonizing memories of his fallen comrades, prepared himself. He felt their spirits rise once again, but not as warriors, but as guides, their strength intertwined with his.

The final confrontation was swift and brutal. The demon's power, already diminished, was no match for the might of the restored locket, coupled with the determination of the boy who had carried their souls, their sacrifices and their memories. With a final, earth-shattering clash, Malkor was vanquished, his power fading back into the abyss from whence it came. The world was safe, but the victory was far from sweet. The weight of sacrifice lay heavy on his heart, and he was left alone, bearing the weight of the world on his shoulders, forever carrying the memories of his fallen companions.

The silence that followed Malkor's demise was deafening, a stark contrast to the cacophony of the battle that had just concluded. A thick pall of smoke hung in the air, obscuring the ravaged landscape. The ground, once fertile and green, was now scarred with fissures and craters, testament to the ferocity of the clash between the demon warlord and the boy who held the souls of five fallen Vikings. Elias stood amidst the devastation, the locket pulsing softly against his chest, its crimson glow a beacon in the smoky gloom. His body ached, his spirit weary, but a profound sense of relief washed over him, a fragile calm amidst the wreckage.

He looked around, searching for his companions. Anya, her face smudged with grime and blood, stumbled towards him, her eyes wide with a mixture of relief and horror. She had sustained multiple wounds during the fight, her armor battered and torn, yet she held herself upright, her strength seemingly defying the gravity of her injuries. Beside her, Ronan, his usually jovial demeanor replaced by a grim solemnity, tended to a grievous wound on his arm. The normally boisterous giant moved with a deliberate slowness, his immense strength now seemingly strained. The weight of the battle, the loss of their friends, was etched deeply on their faces.

Slowly, they began to gather the fallen. The task was grim, each body a reminder of the sacrifice made. Astrid, Leif, Bjorn, and Ragnar lay still, their faces serene in death, their bodies bearing the scars of their final battles. Sven, though wounded critically, was still alive, his breath shallow and ragged. His unwavering faith, the pillar that had sustained him through the darkest moments, had almost broken. Anya and Ronan worked tirelessly, tending to Sven's injuries while Elias, despite his exhaustion, stood watch, his eyes scanning the horizon, his senses alert for any lingering threats.

As they tended to Sven, his eyes flickered open. He looked at each of them, his expression filled with a mixture of pain and quiet acceptance.

He spoke in a barely audible whisper, his voice raspy and weak, yet filled with a quiet strength. "The gods...they...they heard our prayers," he murmured, a faint smile gracing his lips. "But at a cost..." His eyes drifted to the lifeless forms of his comrades, his gaze lingering on each face, his heart evidently breaking.

The ensuing hours were a blur of grief and tending to the wounded. The surviving warriors mourned their lost comrades, sharing stories and memories of the Vikings, their laughter echoing faintly in the stillness. The air throbbed with the echo of the battle, and the loss of their friends. They recounted their triumphs and their failures, their shared hardships and their unbreakable bond. Each story, each memory, was a testament to the strength and courage of those they had lost. The warriors who had fought side-by-side for centuries, their spirits forged in the fires of countless battles, were gone, leaving only the echoes of their strength. Their passing marked not merely an end, but a chapter closed. The weight of their sacrifices was profound, immense and unforgettable.

As the sun began to set, casting long shadows across the ravaged battlefield, they held a small ceremony, a somber farewell to their fallen comrades. They built a pyre from the wreckage of the battle, using broken weapons and shattered armor. Upon it, they placed the bodies of the Vikings, their faces turned towards the setting sun, their spirits set free to journey to Valhalla. The flames consumed the wood, the rising smoke curling into the sky, a final tribute to their heroism, their sacrifice, their eternal bond. Ronan, using his immense strength, lifted a great stone, engraving runes of remembrance in it, setting it as a memorial.

The following days were spent burying the dead and tending to the wounded. The landscape remained a testament to the brutal battle, a grim reminder of the cost of victory. But amidst the devastation, a sense of hope began to emerge. The demon warlord was vanquished. The threat to the kingdom was eliminated. Though the battle had left its scars, a new beginning was within reach.

The victory was bittersweet. Elias, though triumphant, carried a heavy burden. The loss of the Vikings, those who had become more than just spirits within him, left a void within his being that could never truly be filled. Their memories, their experiences, their strength – all were intertwined with his own, and their passing had left him changed, forever marked by their sacrifice. He felt the lingering echoes of their voices, their laughter, their courage, and their final goodbyes. Their battle cries lingered in the silence, reminding him of their sacrifices. He looked at the sky, the setting sun coloring the clouds in shades of orange and crimson, reflecting the locket's glow. The scene mirrored the burning pyre of his Viking friends.

Anya, Ronan, and the few other survivors of the battle rallied around him, their support providing a much-needed anchor. They understood his loss, their own grief intertwining with his. The bond forged in the crucible of battle was stronger than death. This collective grief bound them.

As they began the long process of recovery, of rebuilding both their lives and their kingdom, they knew that the fight was not over. The aftermath of the battle was just the beginning. The victory over Malkor was only a small step in the much larger battle to come. New challenges lay ahead. The scars of the war would remain, and the memory of the fallen Vikings would serve as a constant reminder of the fragility of peace. However, they were together, bound by their common experience, and they stood ready to face whatever challenges the future may hold. They would honor their friends' sacrifices by building a better future. A future worthy of the sacrifices made. A future born from the ashes of a hard-fought battle. A future where their sacrifice had meaning. A new dawn for a new beginning. A new hope for the future.

The final embers of the pyre dwindled, leaving only a bed of glowing coals and the scent of woodsmoke hanging heavy in the air. The wind, whispering through the ravaged landscape, carried the ashes of Astrid, Leif, Bjorn, and Ragnar towards the distant, star-strewn sky. Their souls, released from the burden of the locket, had finally found their rest, their journey concluded. A profound sense of peace, tinged with an unbearable sadness, settled over the survivors. Elias felt it most keenly. The weight that had pressed upon him for so long, the burden of five lives interwoven with his own, had lifted. Yet, the absence left a hollow ache within him, a constant reminder of the bond they had shared, a bond forged in the fires of battle, sealed in blood and sacrifice, and now, tragically severed.

He knelt beside Sven, who lay weakly cradled in Anya's arms. Sven's breathing, once shallow and ragged, now held a steadier rhythm. The wounds, though deep, were slowly healing, aided by Anya's deft hands and Ronan's surprisingly gentle touch. The giant, whose strength was legendary, possessed an unexpected tenderness when caring for the wounded. He hummed a low, mournful tune, a Viking ballad of loss and remembrance, his voice rough but soothing.

Elias reached out, his fingers brushing lightly against Sven's forehead. The locket, still warm against his chest, pulsed faintly, its crimson glow dimming, reflecting the fading embers of the pyre. The magical connection, once a torrent of shared experiences and emotions, had thinned to a gentle stream. He could still feel the faint echoes of their spirits, the whispers of their memories, but they were fading, retreating into the realm of the past. It was a bittersweet farewell, a slow unraveling of a connection that had defined a significant part of his life. It was a profound loss. A heavy one to bear.

As the last vestiges of the Vikings' spirits receded, Elias felt a pang of loss so profound that it nearly brought him to his knees. The transformation that had begun with the locket's awakening had profoundly changed him – physically, mentally, and spiritually. He possessed their strength, their knowledge, their warrior instincts – a legacy he would carry for the rest of his days. Yet, the price of this power had been immense. He had tasted the heights of power and the depths of loss; he had experienced the ecstasy of victory and the agony of grief. He was forever altered by their sacrifice.

Anya gently squeezed his hand, her eyes conveying a silent understanding of his grief. She knew the weight he carried, the burden he bore, not just the physical wounds but also the profound emotional and spiritual scars. Ronan, too, approached, placing a heavy hand on Elias's shoulder. His usual boisterous demeanor was replaced by a somber gravity, reflecting the weight of their shared experience, the shared grief over the loss of their friends. Their bond, forged amidst the tumult of battle, had deepened beyond measure, transcending even the chasm of loss. Their strength was intertwined and interwoven.

The following days were a time for healing and remembrance. The survivors, though physically and emotionally wounded, worked tirelessly to tend to the injured and to bury the dead, both humans and those lost alongside the Vikings. The task was arduous, demanding not just physical strength but also an unwavering spirit. The landscape, scarred by the battle, served as a stark reminder of the brutality of war. But amidst the devastation, the seeds of hope began to take root. The demon warlord was vanquished. The threat that had loomed over the kingdom for so long was finally neutralized. The air, once thick with dread and the stench of decay, now carried the promise of a new beginning.

As the days turned into weeks, the rebuilding began. The people, still shaken but resolute, embarked on the arduous task of repairing their homes, their lives, and their shattered spirits. The rebuilding would take years, but the initial steps were promising. They were unified by their shared trauma, their shared experience, and their shared hope.

Despite the victory, the victory was bittersweet, the triumph laced with an undercurrent of profound loss. The surviving warriors gathered frequently, sharing stories and memories of the Vikings, their laughter often punctuated by tears. Each anecdote, each memory, was a testament to their comrades' courage, their unwavering loyalty, and their unwavering sense of camaraderie. These were not mere warriors, they were friends, brothers and sisters in arms.

Elias found solace in the company of Anya and Ronan. They understood his loss, his pain, and his confusion. Their friendship, solidified by shared trauma, offered him comfort and support in the face of unbearable grief. He found himself increasingly drawn to Anya's strength and resilience, her unwavering determination to rebuild and to restore hope. And Ronan's gentle demeanor, hidden beneath his imposing stature, provided him with an unexpected source of strength and reassurance. They were not merely companions, but family. Their collective strength was palpable. Their bond was unshakeable.

One evening, as the sun dipped below the horizon, painting the sky in hues of fiery orange and crimson, Elias sat alone amidst the ruins of the battlefield. He held the locket in his hand, its crimson glow mirroring the sunset. The magical connection was now almost non-existent. The warriors' spirits, freed from their earthly prison, had departed. Their individual memories had also faded. However, the essence of their strength, their courage, their unwavering spirit—these gifts remained.

He felt their presence, not as distinct personalities, but as a collective force—a powerful echo resonating within his soul. He realized that their sacrifice had not been in vain. They had fought for something greater than themselves, something greater than any individual life, or even for the whole kingdom. They had fought to protect the innocent, to safeguard the future, and to ensure a better tomorrow. And their sacrifice had not been forgotten.

As the stars emerged, glittering against the darkening sky, Elias closed his eyes, his heart filled with a mix of grief and gratitude. He was no longer just Elias; he was Elias, bearing the legacy of five fallen Vikings. He had the strength of their combined souls, their wisdom, their courage. He would honor their memories, not by dwelling on their loss, but by carrying their ideals forward, by working to build a better world, a world worthy of their sacrifice.

The future was yet unwritten. A new beginning for him. A new beginning for them all. A new beginning for the world. A hope for a brighter future was being born. The long, hard road lay ahead, but he was not alone. He had Anya, Ronan, and the memories of the fallen warriors to guide him. And that, he realized, was more than enough. Their journey was over; but his was just beginning. The true battle was yet to begin.

The wind howled a mournful dirge around the crumbling stone tower, mirroring the turmoil within Elias's heart. He stood before Morwen, her once vibrant, terrifying beauty now reduced to a grotesque parody of its former glory. The years, the centuries even, had etched deep lines onto her face, transforming her into a wizened crone, her eyes burning with a desperate, fading fire. The power that had once pulsed from her, the raw, untamed magic that had held the kingdom hostage for centuries, was now a flickering ember, threatening to extinguish altogether.

The battle had been brutal, a whirlwind of spells and steel, of desperate cries and shattering magic. Anya's precise archery, Ronan's raw strength, and Elias's newly found Viking prowess had combined in a perfect storm of coordinated assault. The warriors' spirits, though fading, still lent him their strength, their knowledge of ancient battle strategies, their unyielding spirit in the face of overwhelming odds. He had fought with the ferocity of a berserker, fueled by the memory of Astrid, Leif, Bjorn, and Ragnar, their sacrifices a constant driving force.

Morwen fought with the desperation of a cornered animal. Her spells, once precise and deadly, were now erratic, uncontrolled bursts of chaotic energy that threatened friend and foe alike. Her movements were slow, her reactions sluggish. The centuries of malevolent power had taken their toll. The magic that had sustained her, the dark pact that had given her power over life and death, was cracking under the combined assault of faith, courage and sheer willpower.

It wasn't just their superior fighting skills that had turned the tide; it was the unwavering belief in the righteousness of their cause, a shared faith in the promise of a brighter future. The people, long oppressed under Morwen's tyranny, had rallied to their aid, offering support, providing sanctuary, and bolstering their resolve. They were no longer just fighting for their own survival; they were fighting for the future of their children, their grandchildren – a future free from the shadow of the vengeful sorceress.

As Morwen's power waned, her control over the demonic entities that served her faltered. The grotesque creatures, once fearsome and obedient, now fought among themselves, their loyalty fractured, their allegiance to their dying mistress shattered. The chaos created a narrow window of opportunity, a brief respite that allowed Elias and his companions to push their assault.

The final blow was not delivered by steel or spell, but by a simple, yet profoundly effective act of faith. Anya, drawing upon her own latent magical abilities, and guided by the fading whispers of the Vikings, channeled the collective power of the people, the collective hope for freedom. This wave of collective energy, this unified expression of faith and determination, struck Morwen with the force of a tidal wave, washing away the last remnants of her dark magic, shattering the centuries-old spell that bound her to the kingdom.

Morwen collapsed, her body wracked with spasms, her face contorted in a silent scream of agony and defeat. The darkness that had clung to her for centuries receded, revealing a frail, broken woman, bereft of her power, her influence, her very essence. The air, heavy with the stench of decay and dark magic, began to clear, replaced by the crisp, clean scent of pine and earth.

The silence that followed her collapse was deafening. For a long moment, no one moved, no one spoke, stunned by the magnitude of what had just transpired. The monstrous creatures, their energy source extinguished, crumbled into dust, leaving behind only the faint smell of sulfur and decay. Then, slowly, tentatively, a cheer erupted – a wave of joyous relief that swept across the battlefield, washing away the lingering residue of fear and despair. The kingdom was free.

But the victory was tinged with a bittersweet melancholy. The celebration was muted, tempered by the losses they had suffered. The scars of the battle, both physical and emotional, served as a constant reminder of the cost of freedom. Elias, although victorious, felt the weight of their sacrifice heavily on his shoulders. The echoes of the Vikings' spirits, now almost completely gone, whispered farewell. He knew they were at peace, finally free from their centuries-long torment. Yet, the loss of their presence still left a profound emptiness within him.

Anya approached him, her face etched with concern and affection. She knew his pain, understood the depth of his loss. She placed a comforting hand on his arm, offering a silent reassurance of companionship and support. Ronan, too, moved towards them, his usual boisterous energy tempered by a deep respect for the sacrifice made. His hand rested heavily on Elias's shoulder, a silent acknowledgment of their shared experience, their unwavering bond.

The task of rebuilding lay ahead, a monumental undertaking that would test their courage and resolve. The kingdom was in ruins, its infrastructure shattered, its people traumatized, but their spirit remained unbroken. The seeds of hope, sown amidst the devastation, began to take root. And as they looked towards the future, they carried the memory of the Vikings, their heroism, and their ultimate sacrifice as a testament to the enduring strength of the human spirit.

The subsequent months were a blur of activity. The rebuilding process was arduous, a slow, painstaking effort that involved not just physical labor but also the arduous task of mending broken spirits, healing emotional wounds, and restoring a sense of normalcy. The collective grief transformed into a collective purpose, a shared commitment to building a better future for the kingdom.

Elias, guided by Anya, Finn and Ronan, took on a leadership role, using his newfound strength and Viking knowledge to organize the rebuilding effort. He was no longer just Elias, the outcast, but a leader, a symbol of hope, a beacon of strength in a shattered land. His decisions were guided by the enduring values of the Vikings – courage, loyalty, and unwavering faith in the face of adversity.

He ensured that the fallen were honored, their memories enshrined in stories and songs, their sacrifices immortalized in the hearts of the people. He took solace in Anya's unwavering resilience, her commitment to ensuring a fair and equitable society, a society where everyone had a chance to thrive, regardless of their background or social status. Finn, ever the quiet innovator, dedicated himself to rebuilding the kingdom's infrastructure—designing tools, fortifications, and communication systems that blended ancient rune knowledge with newfound engineering skill. His creations brought both efficiency and hope, reminding the people that progress could rise from ruin. Ronan, with his unwavering loyalty, continued to provide support, ensuring that the people felt safe and protected. The locket, once a source of immense power and turmoil, now lay quietly in Elias's possession, a tangible reminder of his extraordinary journey. The crimson glow had long faded, the magical connection severed. But the essence of the Vikings' strength, their courage, their wisdom, these qualities remained, interwoven into the fabric of his being. As the seasons turned and the kingdom slowly stitched itself back together, the weight of victory gave way to the quiet struggle of endurance. Homes were rebuilt, walls were mended, and fields once scorched by war began to bloom. The people, though scarred, had found hope again. And yet, beneath the celebration and renewal, Elias felt a persistent emptiness—a quiet ache he could not ignore. Sven had not been seen in months.

After surviving the final battle—broken, bloodied, but alive—Sven had drifted in and out of consciousness, his breaths shallow, his voice reduced to a hoarse whisper. He had been tended to with great care by Anya and Ronan, who never left his side during those harrowing days of recovery. But one evening, as twilight spilled gold across the horizon, Elias found Sven alone near the ruins of the pyre, the locket in his trembling hand.

"I'm not whole," Sven had murmured. "Not yet. Not truly." Without waiting for permission, he pressed the locket to his chest. The crimson runes had flickered weakly—like dying embers—before erupting in a brief pulse of light. And then he was gone.

The locket had grown silent again, its glow dim, its presence subdued—but Elias knew. Sven's spirit had returned willingly, not out of duty, but to heal. To rest. Not in death, but in restoration. He was not lost. Just... waiting.

Elias carried that hope with him in the quiet moments, when the world felt too heavy, and the echoes of the Vikings stirred faintly beneath his ribs. Though the others had faded into peace, Sven remained. Not to guide. Not to fight. But to endure. Like the kingdom itself.

As the years passed, the kingdom flourished once more. The scars of the past remained, but they served as a reminder of the resilience of the human spirit and the triumph of good over evil. Elias, Anya, and Ronan, now revered as heroes, continued to lead the kingdom towards a brighter future, their friendship a testament to the power of shared adversity and the unwavering hope that can blossom even in the darkest of times. The new beginning, once a distant dream, had become a tangible reality. The legacy of the Vikings, and the sacrifice they made, would forever be woven into the very tapestry of the kingdom's history, a testament to the enduring power of courage, loyalty, and the unwavering belief in a better tomorrow. Their journey had ended, but the legacy of their sacrifice would live on, a beacon of hope for generations to come.

The air, cleansed of Morwen's malevolent magic, hummed with a newfound vitality. The scent of woodsmoke and freshly turned earth replaced the lingering stench of sulfur and decay. Yet, the victory felt hollow, a fragile peace clinging precariously to the ravaged landscape. The jubilation of freedom was muted, a subdued chorus of relief punctuated by the silent sobs of mourners. The cost of their triumph was etched into the very fabric of the kingdom, visible in the shattered stone of ruined villages, and felt in the empty spaces left by the fallen.

Elias, despite his physical strength enhanced by the Viking spirits, felt the weight of their absence keenly. The echoes of their voices, once a constant source of guidance and power, had faded to a whisper, then silence. The locket, once ablaze with crimson energy, now lay inert against his skin, cold and heavy, a tangible reminder of his extraordinary, and profoundly altering journey. The warriors' spirits, finally free from their centuries-long torment, had departed, leaving behind a void that resonated deep within his soul. He felt a profound loneliness, a stark contrast to the fierce camaraderie he had shared with his Viking companions. Their memories, however, remained, indelibly etched onto his heart and mind.

The physical wounds began to heal. Ronan, with his practical nature and surprisingly deft hands, tended to the injuries of those fortunate enough to survive. Anya, her skills honed by years of tending to her own injuries, moved among the injured, her touch both gentle and assured. She applied herbs and poultices, her knowledge of natural remedies proving invaluable in the absence of proper medical facilities. Their collaborative efforts, a testament to their resilience and their shared bond, eased the physical suffering of the wounded.

But the emotional scars ran deeper. The lingering trauma of the battle, the haunting memories of death and destruction, clung to the survivors like a persistent shadow. Fear gnawed at the edges of their hearts, a constant reminder of the darkness they had barely escaped. Sleep offered no escape; nightmares plagued them, replaying the horrifying scenes of battle, the screams of the dying, the monstrous forms of Morwen's demonic servants. The kingdom, though free, was in ruins, and so too were many of its inhabitants.

The rebuilding began not with mortar and stone, but with words of comfort and acts of compassion. Anya, with her innate understanding of human nature and her fierce determination to create a just and equitable society, organized support groups and created safe spaces where survivors could share their experiences, grieve their losses, and find solace in shared sorrow. Ronan, with his unwavering loyalty and strength, provided both physical and emotional security, ensuring the safety and well-being of those left vulnerable. Elias, though still grappling with his own grief, led by example, offering his strength and unwavering belief in a better future. His presence, his quiet determination, infused a sense of purpose into the dispirited populace.

The physical rebuilding mirrored the emotional one: slow, arduous, and filled with setbacks. Homes were rebuilt, farms were replanted, and broken bridges were slowly repaired. The task was monumental, the scope of the destruction seemingly insurmountable. But the people, inspired by the courage of their leaders and bolstered by a shared sense of purpose, worked tirelessly, their labor fueled by a collective desire to reclaim their lives and their future. Elias drew upon the Vikings' unwavering spirit, their resilience in the face of adversity. He organized the effort, delegating tasks, ensuring fair distribution of resources, and fostering a sense of cooperation that transcended the divisions that had plagued the kingdom for so long.

The process was far from seamless. Arguments arose, frustrations flared, and old resentments resurfaced. But Elias, Anya, Finn and Ronan worked tirelessly to mediate disputes, to foster reconciliation, and to build a society where the past could serve as a lesson, not a source of unending conflict. They learned to listen, to empathize, to bridge the gaps between those who had lost everything and those who had much to give.

As the physical landscape began to heal, so too did the emotional wounds. The laughter of children playing in rebuilt villages began to fill the air, slowly replacing the sounds of mourning. The songs of hope, composed in the aftermath of their victory, were sung by those who had once been too afraid to sing. The collective memory of the battle, though undeniably painful, became a source of shared strength and resilience. They remembered those lost, not with despair, but with gratitude for their sacrifices.

Months turned into years. The scars remained, both physical and emotional, but they served as a constant reminder of the fragility of life and the indomitable strength of the human spirit. Elias, Anya, Finn and Ronan, once outcasts and rebels, became leaders and symbols of hope. Their reign wasn't one of authoritarian rule, but of thoughtful leadership and community building. They focused on creating a system that supported its people and healed the deep wounds of the past. Elias's knowledge of Viking strategies proved invaluable in organizing the rebuilding effort, in distributing resources fairly, and in preventing the exploitation of the vulnerable. He incorporated Viking principles of justice and fairness, ensuring that the kingdom's laws were fair and just, and that those in power acted with responsibility and compassion.

Anya, with her exceptional magical abilities now strengthened by experience, began to teach others, fostering a new generation of healers and mages, empowering individuals to contribute to the rebuilding and healing process. Finn, ever resourceful, focused on restoring infrastructure—developing systems that merged runecraft with technology to help the kingdom run efficiently once more. Ronan, with his unwavering loyalty and strength, continued to protect the kingdom, ensuring its safety from external threats and maintaining order within its borders. The four of them, together, formed a united front against the potential threats that might arise.

The locket remained with Elias, a silent witness to his extraordinary journey. Though its magical power had faded, it served as a powerful reminder of the sacrifices made, the battles fought, and the unwavering spirit that had ultimately prevailed. The memory of the Vikings, their courage, their wisdom, and their selfless sacrifice lived on, not only in Elias's heart, but woven into the very fabric of the kingdom's identity. The new beginning, once a distant dream born amidst despair and chaos, had finally arrived, solidifying itself into a reality filled with the promise of a brighter future. The kingdom, though bearing the scars of war, stood strong, its people unified by shared experience and an unwavering faith in the enduring power of hope and resilience. The past would never be forgotten, but its memory would be woven into the future, a tapestry of strength, resilience, and the enduring human spirit that refuses to bow in the face of adversity. Their journey was far from over, but for now, they stood on the threshold of a new era, embracing the challenges and possibilities that lay ahead.

The kingdom had known peace for several years. Fields once charred by war had bloomed again. The sounds of laughter echoed through village squares. And the once-broken people, though scarred by the past, found strength in each other, in the leadership of Elias, Anya, Ronan, and Finn.

The kingdom itself had changed. Where once stood ruins now stood markets, community centers, training grounds, and temples filled with laughter and devotion. The scent of bread baking wafted through the streets. Children learned to read the runes once lost to time, and elders told stories beneath lantern-lit trees. This peace was hard-earned, and though it brought comfort, the memory of the past never truly left them.

Elias walked often through the villages, not as a ruler, but as a guardian. He helped farmers restore irrigation lines, watched blacksmiths forge tools using ancient Viking designs, and taught warriors to fight not with rage, but with purpose. His eyes often drifted to the locket he still wore, now cool and silent. A reminder. A promise.

Anya, as always, was a force. Her clinics—healing stations built with care—grew into schools of magic and compassion. Children once orphaned by war now studied the art of protective wards and herbal medicine. Her heart had become the pulse of the new society.

Ronan had taken to patrolling the kingdom's borders. His name became legend to would-be raiders, but to his people, he was a gentle giant. He lifted stones, built bridges, and when night fell, told the old Viking ballads to children too afraid to sleep. His grief for the past lived in his silence, but his hope was forged into every action.

And Finn… Finn had become the unlikely architect of a future born of ancient knowledge and innovation. With tools powered by rune circuits and gears, he designed defenses, power sources, and systems to purify water and preserve crops. His hands were often burned, his eyes shadowed by sleepless nights, but he never stopped. The boy who once stood in the background was now the mind behind the kingdom's survival.

Together, they embodied the kingdom's future. Still, even in peace, shadows can grow.

One quiet morning, a cloaked figure stumbled through the eastern gate. Thin, frail, supported by a worn staff of bone-wood and bound with silver thread. He was recognized before he spoke—Professor Alistair. He was gaunt, his robes torn, his eyes haunted. He had traveled through storm and snow, across the Wastes of Eldholt, guided by something beyond knowledge.

"I've returned," he said hoarsely. In his hands, he held a scroll wrapped in cloth, and a shard of luminous rune crystal. "The runes came to me in a dream. Morwen... she lives."

Shock rippled through those gathered. Elias met Alistair's eyes, searching for weakness or madness. He found only fear.

"Explain," Ronan said, stepping protectively in front of a nearby child.

"The final blow destroyed her form, but her essence—the dark soul of Morwen—had already fled. The runes revealed her path. She's hidden in the Deep Vale, where forgotten ley lines pulse with raw magic. And she's not alone."

He unfurled the scroll. Symbols etched in glowing ink danced before their eyes. "She's summoned a demon lord. A creature older than language. Its name has been erased from the runes themselves. Together, they're creating something new. Something worse."

Anya inhaled sharply. "A second war?"

"No," Alistair said, voice trembling. "A reckoning."

Elias felt the locket tremble faintly for the first time in years. He reached for it, eyes narrowing. "We can't wait," he said. "We gather the others. We prepare. The time of rest is over."

They met that evening in the war chamber—a room that had been silent for years, now alight once more. Maps unfurled, old battle plans dusted off. The leaders debated possibilities, evaluated defenses, and sent runners to distant outposts. Alistair spread parchments across the table, tracing ley shifts that mapped to the Deep Vale.

"It's already begun," he said, pointing to a convergence pattern etched in chalk. "This is not just the resurrection of old magic. This is something twisted. The veil between our world and the demon realms is thinning."

"What do they want?" Anya asked.

"To undo the balance," Alistair said. "Not just to conquer, but to erase everything that came before. To rewrite the foundation of magic itself."

Elias stood silently for a long moment. Then, his voice low: "We will not let that happen."

He turned to Ronan. "Rally the border sentries. We may need to evacuate the southern valleys."

"To what end?" Ronan asked.

"To buy us time."

Anya placed her hand over the rune map. "Then we find the source and destroy it before it breaks into our world."

Finn, quiet until now, spoke up. "I'll need time to reconfigure the pulse trackers. If the demon lord is affecting ley lines, I can trace the distortion."

Elias nodded. "Do it. We strike before they rise."

And so, the kingdom prepared for a war it had once believed finished. The peace had been a dream. Now, reality called them back to the edge.

The sky above the ruins of the First Temple rippled with early morning mist as Elias approached the sacred grounds with Anya, Ronan, and Finn. The ruins, once a place of chaos and raw energy, had since been transformed into a sanctified site of remembrance and magical potential. Over the years, it had become a quiet sanctuary, watched over by acolytes and guarded by the elemental wards Anya had woven into its boundaries.

Today, however, the ruins pulsed again with a faint promise of power. The magical stone Elias had unearthed years ago rested at the heart of the site, dormant but whole. Cracks in its surface shimmered faintly, as if aware of what was coming.

The group had assembled in silence. Elias had not summoned Sven in years—not since the locket's final glow had dimmed. But as the threat returned, so too did the need for the spirits who had once saved the realm.

He knelt in the center of the stone ring and placed the locket on the platform etched with the runes of binding. "Sven," he whispered, the name itself heavy with longing and hope.

The locket vibrated. A pulse of red light shimmered outward. A wind stirred through the ruins. The light flickered like flame, and slowly, a figure stepped from its center. Sven's spectral form appeared, more refined than the last time they had seen him—his armor gleamed with ghostly silver, and his face carried a gravity that only centuries of wisdom could forge.

"I felt it," Sven said before anyone could speak. "She's moving. The shadows are stirring."

Elias stood. "Can you bring them back?"

Sven turned to the stone. "Yes. The others are ready. They've waited beyond the veil, prepared to return. But we must be careful. This time, the bridge will not be as forgiving."

Finn stepped forward, producing a glyph-board wrapped in copper veins. "I've integrated the old binding patterns into this design. It should stabilize the magic and allow for longer manifestation. The stone reacts to both runes and memory, so focus will be key."

Anya moved to the outer circle, anchoring warding points and grounding crystals. "I'll maintain balance. Any disruption and we'll lose the connection."

Sven began to chant. The runes carved into the stone ring glowed to life. His words—ancient and resonant—reverberated through the air like thunder layered in music. The sky darkened slightly. Wind rushed inward, then upward.

"Ragnar," Elias called. "Leif. Bjorn. Harald. Astrid."

Each name was a beacon.

A second wave of energy exploded from the locket. Light cracked through the sky like a sunrise bursting from beneath the earth. The ground trembled beneath their feet. Energy funneled through the stone and up into the air. It was like the world itself held its breath.

Then—one by one—they returned.

Astrid stepped forth first. Her form glowed with radiant energy, her shield etched with runes anew. Ragnar came next, his face marked by wisdom and fire. Leif emerged beside him, bow already drawn and eyes narrowed in resolve. Bjorn's steps thundered like rolling boulders, his axe gleaming with spiritual flame. Last came Harald, silent and radiant, a cloak of starlight trailing from his shoulders.

The Vikings circled Elias and bowed.

"We've waited," Ragnar said. "Now we rise again."

Sven collapsed to one knee, panting from the exertion. Elias reached out and helped steady him.

"The connection is not permanent," Sven warned. "Their time here is tied to the stone and the strength of our cause. But they are here, Elias. They are with you."

A ripple of relief and purpose washed over Elias. The old flame reignited in his chest.

"They will not rise without opposition," Finn muttered. "Blackspire will not fall easily."

"Then we won't give it the chance to stand," Anya said, eyes flashing.

Elias nodded, looking around at his companions—spiritual and physical alike.

"Gather what you need," he said. "We move before the shadows rise further."

Together, they turned toward the horizon, the Vikings flanking them like guardians of legend returned.

The old world had called them back.

And they would answer.

The journey to Blackspire Keep was grueling. For days, the group traveled through gnarled forests and scorched valleys, the land growing darker and more corrupted with every mile. Once vibrant wildlife had vanished, replaced by shriveled trees and whispers that danced on the wind like voices from forgotten nightmares.

Elias led with a quiet intensity, the locket against his chest humming faintly, reacting to the pulsing dark magic ahead. Astrid and Ragnar moved like sentinels on either side, silent but alert, their spectral forms shimmering beneath the overcast sky. Anya rode beside Elias, her eyes constantly scanning the horizon for signs of movement, while Ronan and Finn brought up the rear, carrying supplies and tracking magical shifts with rune-tuned instruments.

Blackspire Keep emerged from the mist like a monument to despair. The fortress loomed high above the valley floor, its blackened stone towers clawing at the heavens. Lightning danced between spires that appeared to hum with life. The air reeked of sulfur, blood, and corruption. It wasn't just a fortress—it was a wound in the world.

From a ridge above, Elias studied the keep's defenses. Massive walls were covered in writhing glyphs. At the gate, statues of horned beasts guarded the entrance—stone sentinels with empty eye sockets that seemed to watch every movement. The landscape surrounding the keep was a killing field: charred bones, broken siege engines, and scorched earth marked failed attempts at assault from long ago.

Ronan exhaled deeply. "We're walking into death's throne room."

"Then we make death remember who we are," Elias replied.

The group descended the ridge under the cover of a spell Anya had woven—shadows clung to their cloaks, muting sound and scent. At the gates, they paused.

Finn extended a hand. "Give me one minute."

He knelt and pressed a rune-carved device into the ground. Blue sparks leapt from stone to soil. The glyphs on the gate flickered. Then, with a groan like metal twisting in agony, the defenses flickered—just long enough for Ronan to drive his shoulder into the gate, splintering the weakened lock.

Inside, the keep came alive.

The halls were black stone, alive with demonic energy. Torches burned green, casting long shadows that slithered across the walls. The air buzzed with whispering voices—fragments of incantations, screams of the damned, and guttural laughter.

They moved as one. Bjorn took point, his massive shield absorbing incoming strikes from shadowy creatures that lunged from the walls—twisted, malformed things with too many limbs and eyes that bled light. Astrid and Leif provided cover fire with ice-tipped arrows and wind-laced spears, while Harald wove protective barriers that shimmered like silver fog.

Each hallway was a battlefield.

In one corridor, they were ambushed by hulking brutes covered in armor fused with flesh. Elias faced one head-on. Sword met claw, sparks flying as steel clashed against corruption. The locket pulsed, and Elias felt the presence of his Viking spirits guiding him, pushing his reflexes beyond mortal bounds. He struck with precision, remembering Astrid's training, Bjorn's strength, and Sven's agility.

In the chapel, desecrated and turned into a shrine of agony, Anya faced a dark priestess—once human, now more shadow than substance. They exchanged spells, fire and frost erupting through stained glass and fractured pews. Anya summoned a storm of light, searing the darkness away. When it was done, she stood alone, panting, her eyes glowing with inner fire.

Finn sabotaged summoning circles etched into the stone floor, carving his own runes in counter-formation, redirecting magic back into the keep's foundations. When one circle erupted prematurely, he shielded Ronan with a barrier of reinforced glyphwork, earning a rare nod from the warrior.

As they approached the inner sanctum, the keep shook. Alarms howled in forgotten tongues. The sky outside bled red.

Finally, they reached the throne room.

Morwen waited.

She stood at the center of a circular platform etched with thousands of glowing runes, all leading inward toward a pulsing rift in the ground. The demon lord stood behind her—twenty feet tall, his form wreathed in fire and shadow, his face hidden beneath a bone crown. Chains of molten gold wrapped around his limbs, anchoring him to the ritual's heart.

"Welcome, heroes," Morwen said, her voice echoing unnaturally. Her eyes glowed with the promise of death. "You're just in time to witness your failure."

Elias stepped forward. "We've ended you once. We'll do it again."

She laughed. "You ended a vessel. I am reborn. My lord has shown me what true power is."

The ritual surged. The floor cracked. Energy coiled upward.

Astrid and the Vikings surged forward. Anya unleashed a volley of arrows into the ritual field, aiming for the runes that held the demon lord. Ronan and Elias charged together, striking at the barriers protecting Morwen.

The battle was chaos. Harald held off waves of summoned demons with a dome of celestial energy. Bjorn's shield shattered under a brute's blow, yet he fought on, fist and steel driving enemies back. Finn directed energy spikes from the keep's own defenses into the ritual ring.

Every spell, every swing of a sword felt like a prayer.

The demon lord roared, breaking a portion of his bindings.

Astrid screamed a warning, hurling her staff with all the force of the spirit realm behind it. It struck the demon's shoulder, buying them seconds.

Morwen raised her hands and called the final rune into place.

The ground split open.

The spell completed. A thunderous pulse of magic rippled across the chamber like a shockwave from the gods themselves. The air grew thick—oppressive, almost sentient—as seven ancient runes ignited in a perfect circle around the central ritual site. Each rune burned with a distinct hue: crimson, emerald, obsidian, gold, violet, icy blue, and sickly green. Together, they formed a halo of primal power—seven flames licking hungrily at the veil between worlds.

Elias stepped back instinctively, the locket on his chest glowing violently. He knew—without question—that they had failed.

Cracks spiderwebbed outward from the runes. Lava surged from the fractures, steam hissing as fire met ancient stone. The stench of brimstone filled the air, followed by the sound of something... breathing. Something old.

From the depths, seven spirits rose—one from each rune. They didn't move so much as they *unfolded*, pulled from the bones of the earth itself, drawn upward on tendrils of dark magic and twisted desire.

They did not speak. They simply existed—and their presence alone bent the world around them.

Pride emerged first, cloaked in velvet shadows and adorned in gold. His crown was fused to his skull, his spine perfectly straight. He floated above the ground, arms outstretched as if the world should kneel before him. The air around him shimmered with illusion and grandeur.

Greed slithered next, its form constantly shifting—growing, consuming, multiplying. Coins and gems poured from its fingertips and then dissolved into nothing. Its mouth stretched into a cruel grin as it reached toward the light, always grasping, never satisfied.

Envy came crawling, dragging itself with elongated limbs and dagger-like fingers. It hissed in jealousy, its eyes reflecting the faces of those it beheld. It mimicked them, twisted them, became them— only to discard the forms in frustration.

Wrath burst from the molten core like an explosion. A humanoid inferno, its eyes were twin suns of fury. Every step it took scorched the stone, every breath a growl of war. It roared, and the walls of the chamber trembled in response.

Sloth rose slowly, dripping shadow like tar. Its limbs sagged, but its aura was heavy—so heavy that it dragged energy, light, and hope into a void of apathy. Even Ronan staggered under its presence, his strength dulled by the pull of nothingness.

Gluttony followed, gurgling laughter spilling from a mouth that multiplied with each breath. It oozed across the stone, its massive form a writhing mass of hunger, its voice a grotesque song of indulgence and excess.

And then came **Lust**. Beautiful, terrible, a constantly shifting figure of impossible allure. Eyes like twin galaxies, lips that whispered false promises. Wherever it turned, even the shadows leaned closer.

One by one, they lifted from the stone and rose into the sky, their bodies dissipating into trails of corrupted magic, streaking across the heavens like falling stars in reverse.

Elias fell to his knees, his hand gripping the edge of the ritual circle. The locket on his chest dimmed, sputtered, and went silent.

"We failed," he whispered. His voice was not broken—but hollow. The kind of emptiness born from watching your greatest fear made manifest.

Across the room, Morwen laughed—not with malice, but with vindication. Her form shimmered and cracked, her skin flaking to ash, her voice fading even as it rang triumphant. "You delayed me once. But you cannot stop what is eternal."

Then, she crumbled, her final breath a curse in a forgotten tongue.

The Demon Lord behind her rumbled, its molten chains evaporating. Its essence, its purpose, had been fulfilled. It turned toward Elias for a moment—silent, almost... amused—and then its form collapsed inward, imploding into a void of fire and dust.

Silence.

The chamber, once alive with heat and chaos, fell into a stillness so complete it pressed on the ears. Astrid stepped forward. Her spirit form flickered from exertion but stood tall. "Then we hunt them," she said. "Each one."

Ragnar nodded, already tightening the strap on his axe. "If they've been loosed upon the world, then the world needs us more than ever."

Leif stepped to Elias's side, offering a steadying hand. "This is not defeat. It's the beginning of the true battle."

Anya knelt beside Elias, placing a hand over his. Her voice was quiet but certain. "You don't carry this alone."

Ronan sheathed his weapon with deliberate force. "Let them run. We'll find them."

Finn closed the tattered remnants of his rune map and added, "I'll track the ley distortions. They won't stay hidden."

Elias rose slowly. The locket was cold now, but his heart pulsed with fire.

"We faced death. We survived. We stood against gods and monsters," he said. "Now we stand against sin itself."

They left the chamber in silence. Not in mourning, but in preparation. The sky above Blackspire burned with streaks of unnatural color—each one a path taken by a spirit of corruption.

The map of their next journey had been carved into the sky. But the true story of The Soulbound Curse had only just begun.

Acknowledgments

First and foremost, I extend my deepest gratitude to my family, my wife, Loretta and all of my kids and friends, whose unwavering support and endless patience made this book possible. Their belief in me, even during moments of self-doubt, fueled my creativity and kept me going through the long writing process. A special thanks goes to Regal Insight Consulting, whose insightful feedback and meticulous editing were invaluable in shaping the final manuscript.

J.B. Grimm is a fiction and fantasy author with a lifelong passion for storytelling. Their love for epic high fantasy, infused with elements of dark fantasy and historical fiction, is evident in their work. He draws inspiration from classic authors like Tolkien and Rowling, and aims to create richly detailed worlds with memorable characters and compelling narratives. J. B. Grimm's work explores themes of courage, resilience, and the enduring power of hope in the face of adversity. Beyond writing, he enjoys spending quality time with his wife and many children, inventing, working on cars and diesel engines and sharing his love with CDL Drivers.

www.ingramcontent.com/pod-product-compliance
Lightning Source LLC
Chambersburg PA
CBHW071528100726
47908CB00004B/1324